MURDER AT THE ABBEY

FRANCES EVESHAM

Boldwood

First published in Great Britain in 2021 by Boldwood Books Ltd.

A CIP catalogue record for this book is available from the British Library.

Paperback ISBN 978-1-80048-055-1

Hardback ISBN 978-1-80280-979-4

Large Print ISBN 978-1-80048-054-4

Ebook ISBN 978-1-80048-057-5

Kindle ISBN 978-1-80048-056-8

Audio CD ISBN 978-1-80048-049-0

MP3 CD ISBN 978-1-80048-050-6

Digital audio download ISBN 978-1-80048-051-3

Boldwood Books Ltd
23 Bowerdean Street
London SW6 3TN
www.boldwoodbooks.com

To Chris, Pippa and Nick with love.

1

Libby Forest groaned as she hitched her backpack higher. 'Are we nearly there, yet? I'm roasting.'

Max Ramshore threw a stick for Shipley the springer spaniel to fetch. 'Almost. And these packs weigh a ton. I blame you, of course. They're full of your food.'

Libby snorted. 'Nonsense. It's all the beer you brought. My creations are as light as a feather. At least, that's what you said before I married you.'

Shipley returned, somehow looking pleased with himself despite the stick in his mouth.

'He doesn't seem to feel the heat at all, does he?' Libby said, pulling a treat from a pocket. Shipley dropped the stick and crunched the chicken flavoured treat. 'I'm glad we left Bear at home,' Libby went on. 'It would be far too hot for him today and his rheumatic joints would suffer. And,' she spoke in mock severity, 'please don't offer a scientific description of how a Carpathian Sheepdog's thick fur wicks away sweat and stops him from overheating.'

'Yes, dear,' Max said, meekly. 'Married six months and you're bullying me already.' He stopped walking. 'Come over here, there's a nice patch of shade under this tree.'

'Six months already,' Libby repeated, allowing him to fold her in his arms. She broke into tuneless song. 'And it don't seem a day too long.'

Max chuckled. 'I was terrified something would go wrong at the wedding – that you'd be kidnapped or my ex-wife would turn up with yet another toy boy. But it was perfect, wasn't it?'

'Everything I'd dreamed about. You, me, the children and both dogs. Although I think Fuzzy felt left out.'

'Cats don't like weddings.'

A voice behind them interrupted, 'Mrs F., get a room, please.' Mandy, Libby's tenant in Hope Cottage, had caught up.

'Nothing to see here,' Max said.

Libby linked her arm in Max's as they walked on. 'You know, Mandy, you could call me Libby.'

Max mumbled, 'If you'd agreed to take my name, she could call you Mrs R. instead.'

'I'm much too old to change my name,' Libby pronounced, as though they hadn't enjoyed this argument a hundred times, 'and we'd also have to change the name of our private investigation business to Ramshore and Ramshore, which would just be silly. Not to mention altering the labels for Mrs Forest's Chocolates.'

'Which is a successful brand,' Mandy pointed out.

Libby asked, 'Aren't you hot?' Despite the unusual heat of the last few June days, Mandy wore a black maxi dress under a red lace shawl.

'Cotton and lace, that's the answer.' Mandy, Libby's talented and capable assistant, was also a determined Goth, buying most of her clothes at vintage shops in Bristol and Bath and wearing an ever-changing supply of metal face adornments. Today's addition was a third silver ring through her right eyebrow. 'And here's my secret weapon.' With a flourish, she pulled out a black lace fan from one of the pockets of the voluminous dress and waved it in front of her face, her armful of chain-mail bracelets clinking musically. 'Anyway, we've arrived.'

They rounded a clump of trees and Cleeve Abbey, the twelfth-century Cistercian abbey, this year's destination for the Exham-on-Sea History Society's picnic, rose before them, semi-ruined but still exuding an air of gentle rural calm.

With relief, they chose a spot in the shade of the majestic trees within the abbey walls and dropped their backpacks on the grass. Libby spread a checked cloth on the grass and Max peeped into a series of sealed containers stuffed with tiny goats' cheese and onion filo tartlets, smoked salmon and beetroot baguettes, a selection of salads and individual jars of strawberry cheesecake.

'No chocolate today, I'm afraid. Not in this heat,' Libby said.

Soon, the other members of the society arrived. Some had left cars across the lane, while others had followed the example of Libby, Max and Mandy and taken the steam train to nearby Washford Station, walking the last half-mile to the abbey.

They bought guidebooks from the shop and wandered happily through the well-preserved ruins, exclaiming at the preservation of the indoor areas, soaking up the atmosphere of peace and tranquillity in the cloister, and chatting with a couple of knowledgeable volunteers.

An hour later, Libby lay supine with her head in Max's lap, her stomach comfortably full, enjoying the warmth of the dappled sunlight on her face. Nearby, a cow lowed, contented. Rooks cawed from the tops of the trees. Peering through her sunglasses, Libby spotted a skylark rising, singing its heart out, until it was a tiny dot in the perfect azure sky.

'You know,' she murmured, 'that Caribbean island was a great place for our honeymoon, and sunshine in January was a wonderful treat, but there's nothing to beat a beautiful summer day in Somerset.' She sat up. 'In fact, that must be why it's called Somerset. I hadn't thought of that, before.'

Quentin Dobson, folded like a spider into a camping chair nearby, turned and smiled. Elderly but still spry, the curator of the museum at nearby Watchet could never resist an opportunity to pass on what he called 'fun facts' from his remarkable fund of historical knowledge. 'As you would expect,' he began, settling his wire-rimmed spectacles more comfortably over his ears, 'Somerset originally referred to "people who live near Somerton", with Somerton meaning a summer settlement. I believe it was the Celts, looking across from Wales, who originally named it in honour of the green fields they could see across the Bristol Channel. But I'm afraid I can't remember the attribution, just now, so perhaps it would be best not to quote me.'

Max nudged Libby. 'No danger of that,' he whispered, as Jemima Bakewell, a retired, unmarried school teacher with a passion for history, offered an alternative theory. Something about mispronunciation – Libby really didn't care. It was far too hot to worry.

She watched as Max listened to the earnest conversation with a puzzled frown. He maintained a love-hate relationship with the History Society, for he lacked the members' enthusiasm for gossip. Libby had shamelessly dangled the chance to drink his favourite Hook Norton beer in the sun as a bribe to get him to today's picnic.

The society members finished eating and Dr Archie Phillips, the aging librarian at Wells Cathedral, rose and stretched. 'Time for a little exercise,' he said. 'Jemima, come for a stroll?' He'd driven Jemima Bakewell to the picnic himself, claiming the right to set her chair close to his. He'd seemed none too pleased when Quentin joined them.

Jemima stood awkwardly, leaning on the flimsy arm of her chair. It tipped sideways and only Archie's supporting arm saved her from a fall. 'Oops.' She blushed. 'I'm always falling over. It's a good thing no one expects me to wear stilettos like the young folks. I'd be on the floor all the time.' Giggling like a teenager after her two glasses of white wine, she set off towards the river, Archie at her side.

Mandy slipped a slice of ham to Shipley. 'I think it's adorable,' she said. 'At their age.'

'What do you mean by that, young lady?' Quentin, older than either Jemima or Archie, had overheard.

'Sorry,' Mandy grinned, not at all apologetic. 'I just think it's lovely when older people get together. You know, for companionship or whatever.'

Quentin's face was beetroot red. 'Good gracious me, you young people think life ends at fifty. Ridiculous.' Snorting like a horse, he left his chair and followed Jemima and Archie.

Libby wagged a finger at Mandy. 'We'll throw you out of the society if you're cheeky,' she said.

'I don't mean you two,' Mandy said. 'You're quite sprightly, really. But Jemima must be, like, over seventy, and Quentin's even older. I mean, can they even—'

A cry from the river saved her from digging a bigger hole for herself.

'Oh no. What's Jemima done now?' sighed Libby's friend, Angela Miles. 'Do you think we should find out?' She rose, gracefully, from a velvet cushion. Trust Angela, Libby thought fondly, to somehow contrive to look elegant even at a picnic.

Mandy chuckled. 'Maybe those two are fighting over her.'

Just then, Archie returned, purple from running, beckoning frantically. 'Come here, everyone. You'll never believe what we've found.'

2

THE FIND

Galvanised, the picnickers ran towards the river, Shipley bounding by Libby's side, straining at the leash. The water gurgled happily over stones, beside the lane and just outside the remains of the abbey walls. Jemima stood in the river, the water reaching halfway up her calves, and tugged at something under the waterline.

'What is it?' Libby cried.

'You'll never believe it. I saw it sticking out of the bank.'

Quentin hovered at the edge of the water. 'I told you not to go in the water. You'll catch your death.'

'Nonsense. It's refreshing.' Jemima gave another tug, whatever she was holding came away from the mud of the bank with a squelch, and she toppled backwards into the river, waving a pale object above her head. 'Got it,' she shouted.

Archie tried to help her out of the water, but she brushed him away. 'Stop fussing and look what I found.'

In her right hand, one end clogged with mud, the other washed clean by the water, she held a long, pale bone.

'Oh, Good Lord,' Angela breathed. 'Please, tell me it's an animal.'

The society members jostled each other, keen to get a closer look.

Quentin took the bone from Jemima's hand. 'If I'm not mistaken,' he intoned, solemnly, 'this is a human thigh bone.'

Max hovered on the edge of the river, straining to get a better look. 'I can't see any more—'

A shout interrupted him. 'Oi. You lot. What are you up to? You can't fish in this river, not without a permit, you know.'

Libby turned and her stomach lurched. She recognised the man appearing from a clump of trees between the river and the abbey. Her throat tight, she gasped, 'Max, it's Wendlebury. Chesterton Wendlebury.' She grabbed Max's hand, squeezing it. 'He's back.'

Wendlebury, over six feet tall and as broad as a weightlifter, shook a carved walking stick at the picnickers as he advanced, red-faced and angry. His hair was thinner than last time Libby had seen him in Taunton Crown Court, where he'd been sentenced for his very minor role as a bumbling board member of a fraudulent organisation, Pritchards, in a case that had rocked Exham-on-Sea to its foundations.

'Well, if it isn't Mrs Forest. Good afternoon to you, dear lady,' Wendlebury boomed. 'And is this by any chance one of the Exham societies you all love so much, enjoying a day out? And what on earth have you got there?'

Libby swallowed, but before she could speak, Max replied, 'Wendlebury, fancy meeting you here. Good to see you out and about again.'

Quentin's eyes narrowed. 'We're not fishing, and in any case the river doesn't belong to you. So we'd be grateful if you'd leave us to our business.'

Archie nodded in agreement, and turned to Jemima. 'Besides, we must call the authorities and find out whether or not this bone is human.'

Jemima waded carefully out of the river, clutching Archie's arm for support, as Quentin laid the trophy reverently on the grass. Wendlebury's arrival had silenced the members of the society, but now their voices rose in a babble of excited comment.

Under cover of the chatter, Libby whispered in Max's ear, 'I know it's silly, but seeing Wendlebury again gives me the shivers. I knew he was coming out of prison, but to meet him brings it all back.' Chesterton Wendlebury's company had been involved in the death of Libby's first husband a few years ago, shortly before she moved to Exham-on-Sea. Though Trevor had been an overbearing and controlling man and had played a part in the money-laundering scam, he hadn't deserved to die.

'No need to worry,' Max said, giving her shoulder a reassuring squeeze. 'Wendlebury was more a fool than a criminal. Weak, rather than bad, despite his bluster.'

'Just so long as history doesn't repeat itself,' Libby muttered.

They turned their backs on Wendlebury and peered at the long, strong bone.

'Are there any more in there?' Angela asked.

Max turned to Mandy. 'Could you run up to reception? They'll call the police and contact experts if it looks like a human bone—'

'Which it certainly does,' Libby put in.

'I'm going to see if there are any more in the river,' Jemima interrupted. She shook off Archie's arm and stepped back into the water. 'It's just as well it's summer.'

Libby, distracted by a series of shudders that had run down her back at the sight of Chesterton Wendlebury, had dropped

Shipley's lead. Before she could stop him, he leapt into the water and nosed along the bank.

'There,' said Jemima. 'He's come to help. A grand fellow, aren't you? Now, what can we find?'

Libby shared a despairing look with Max as Shipley, suddenly rigid and pointing to show he'd found something interesting, gave a short, sharp bark.

'There's more.' Jemima was triumphant. She scraped away more mud as the others gathered round. Slowly, under her fingers, a smooth, rounded bone appeared.

Libby recognised it. 'Wait,' she called. 'I don't think we should disturb it. You can see – it's—'

Max put his arm around her shoulders. 'It's a human skull.'

Silence fell.

Archie's voice sounded strained, 'It may not be human...' and faded into silence.

The watchers exchanged glances, quite certain they were looking at the remains of a person.

Mandy returned with a guide. 'The police are on their way,' she said. 'They sound thrilled. I guess they haven't had much excitement since that last murder in the Avon Gorge.'

The elation of the find had ebbed away and, as if on cue, clouds began to gather in the sky. Jemima, back on dry land once more, shivered.

'It's going to rain,' Quentin said. 'We should find shelter. The police could take hours to get here.'

'Well, I'm going nowhere,' Jemima said. 'We can stay dry in the abbey – in the refectory or the dormitory.'

Finally, after discussion, Libby, Max and the guide agreed to stay down by the river with the bones while the others, refusing to leave until they'd squeezed every drop of interest out of the day, wandered back to the abbey to finish eating and take shelter from the approaching weather.

Archie insisted on leading Jemima to his car, to keep her warm.

Mandy hissed at Libby, 'He'll be telling her to take off her dress and wrapping her in a blanket.'

Libby gestured towards Quentin. 'Not if he has anything to do with it.'

'Do you think they'll fight?' Mandy's eyes gleamed.

'I think there's been quite enough excitement for one day,' Libby said, firmly. To her relief, Chesterton Wendlebury had left the scene. Not in a hurry to meet up with the boys in blue again, Libby guessed. 'I wonder how it was that Wendlebury appeared just then. Was he following us?' she asked Max.

He shrugged. 'I've no idea. I suppose he's just out for a day in the countryside. Once the police arrive, we should get on home. Shipley needs a bath – he's covered in mud.'

3

MONKS

Next morning, Libby's phone rang even before she was dressed.

A young voice said, 'Detective Constable Gemma Humberstone here. Detective Chief Inspector Morrison suggests that, as you were present at Cleeve Abbey yesterday, when those bones were found, perhaps you'd like to come and meet with the biological anthropologist today.'

'Come again, Gemma,' Libby yawned. 'It's far too early for long words.' As a partner in Ramshore and Forest, Private Investigators, she'd worked closely with Gemma on other murder inquiries. Despite the young constable's initial reluctance to work with an amateur investigator, the two women had learned to like and trust each other.

'She's a bone expert,' Gemma explained. 'She works at Bristol University and she's going to the abbey to excavate the bones from the Washford River. We sent a photo, and she agrees they're likely to be human, in which case they have to be treated with great care, examined and then reburied even if they're ancient bones. We're hoping she'll know how old they are, although she says it will take a while and we're not to expect a quick result.'

'We'll be there.' Libby couldn't wait. Since the day she found a body under the nine-legged lighthouse on Exham-on-Sea beach, she'd discovered a talent for sleuthing. A frisson of excitement slid down her spine. Was this going to be another twisty, intricate investigation into murder, or was there a prosaic explanation?

Gemma told her not to bring the entire History Society, but agreed Jemima, Quentin and Archie were welcome as they'd found the bones. Max and Libby, she pointed out, were invited because DCI Morrison paid a tiny retainer fee to them as Ramshore and Forest, Private Investigators, to help in occasional cases.

'Which gives Morrison priority access to us,' Max pointed out, grimacing at himself in his shaving mirror as Libby recounted the phone conversation

She laughed. 'Sounds grand, though, doesn't it? Makes us sound like proper private investigators. Not that the pet owners who employ us privately to find their cats and dogs care about that.'

'Well, unless we go down the road of spying on cheating husbands and wives, pet owners and the police are our major client groups. Your baking and chocolates are far more profitable than the PI work, of course.' He paused, turned and plonked a foamy kiss on Libby's cheeks. 'And far tastier, if a little decadent.' He patted his paunch.

She wiped away his shaving foam. 'I bought you a top-of-the-range electric razor, but you never use it,' she complained.

'No, I like a proper shave from a decent blade. Feel that.' He proffered his chin for Libby to stroke. 'See what I mean? Smooth as a baby's bottom.'

Libby sat on their bed, watching as he finished shaving. Sometimes, she could hardly believe they'd only been married for six months. It felt as though they'd been together for ever, they fitted so well. She even enjoyed their arguments. There were plenty of those. A few days ago, they'd argued for twenty minutes over the best way to load the dishwasher. Both forthright souls, they'd each expected to be living out the second halves of their lives as singletons and as a result, as she'd admitted to Max, they were set in their ways. 'But at least we enjoy making up afterwards.'

For the thousandth time, Libby gave thanks for her decision to move to Exham-on-Sea when her first husband died. She shivered. She could be living in London, alone and lonely, if she hadn't decided she needed a change of direction. She still had friends there, kept in touch with them and visited occasionally, but they'd known her as half a couple when she was married to Trevor. She'd been determined to brush the dust of London off her feet and move to the calm of England's West Country when Trevor died. Not that life had stayed calm. The last few years had been a whirl of excitement, culminating in her wedding to Max last Christmas.

There was something about this part of the world. Exham-on-Sea was a mix of people. Many had grown up there and never left, while others had come on holiday, loved the fresh sea air and miles of sand and returned later to live there. Even Libby's two children, who'd tried at first to persuade her against the move, had gradually joined her. Robert, her son, lived nearby with his wife, Sarah, who was pregnant – very pregnant – with their first child. To Libby's delight, her wayward daughter Ali was now in Exham too, albeit temporarily, before returning to Brazil with her boyfriend, to train as a doctor.

'Well,' Max said, now fully dressed. 'The sun's shining, so get some of your oldest clothes on in case we end up scrambling about in the river. Judging from what we could see of that bone, at least we aren't looking at a recent death.'

'Funny, that.' Libby paused, one arm in a trusty old mud-coloured linen T-shirt. 'You'd think one death was as bad as another, but if this bone's as old as we think, it's not so sad, somehow. It's more exciting than upsetting, although seeing the skull gave me a jolt. I wonder what stories the bones will tell.'

The old grandfather clock in Max's study clanged nine times.

'Let's get going,' Libby said. 'I've got a busy day and I don't want to neglect baking too much. After all, that's how I made my living when I arrived in Somerset. I promised to call into Hope Cottage this afternoon, to work on some new recipes with Mandy. She does most of the baking in the café's kitchen, but I like to work with her on new products and Angela's begging for more.'

Max said, 'Angela's turned out to be quite a stern taskmaster since she opened the new café.'

'She's in her element,' Libby agreed. 'The Crusts and Crumbs Café gets busier every day, and now the summer season's in full swing, the tills ring constantly.' She retrieved a pair of sturdy boots from the wardrobe. 'Metaphorically, I mean. Most people just tap credit cards, which is efficient but far less cheery.'

Max ran downstairs, collected Bear and Shipley, and loaded them into his car. Fuzzy, Libby's fat and lazy marmalade cat, stalked past the two dogs with her usual supercilious air and made her way to the sunniest spot in Max's study, where she stretched out, sighed deeply as though pleased to have the house to herself, and went to sleep.

4

BONES

The section of Washford River that ran past the abbey was cordoned off with police tape in case it should turn out to be what DC Gemma Humberstone called 'a forensic case of interest to the police'. Libby supposed that meant an unexplained and possibly recent death.

When she arrived, a small group of young people, probably students from Bristol University, were already squatting at the water's edge holding trowels. As well as observers from the English Heritage Trust, the organisation caring for the abbey, a group of sightseers had gathered nearby, alerted by Somerset Live online news. In addition, the three History Society members were easy to spot, for they were holding forth to a group of ramblers who'd come across the site on their way around the Coast Path from Minehead to Bridgwater.

Jemima, eyes gleaming with the joy of a lifelong teacher, was explaining the history of the area to the newcomers. She seemed to have covered several centuries before Libby's arrival, from the Bronze Age to the Reformation and the dissolution of the monasteries. Some of the ramblers' eyes had glazed over. Others leaned around Jemima's considerable bulk, trying to see what the handful of workers inside the police cordon were doing.

Max and Libby approached the dig, both dogs held firmly on leads, and Libby's heart sank. 'Oh no,' she murmured. 'PC Ian Smith.'

Max squeezed her hand. 'Might have known he'd be here. He's dead wood in DCI Morrison's team and kept away from anything sensitive. Morrison would see an archaeological dig as a safe place, where Smith can't cause trouble.'

Spotting them approaching, PC Smith raised the tape to let them through. 'Can't imagine you'll have much to say about this case,' he sneered at Libby. 'Seems to be ancient history. Though, mind you...' his gaze travelled, insultingly, over her face.

Max took a long step and got between Smith and Libby. 'Got something to say, Smith?' he asked.

Smith shrugged. 'Just trying to be friendly.' He gave a false smile, his tiny eyes almost disappearing in a pudgy face.

DC Gemma Humberstone raised her eyebrows at Libby. 'Sorry about Ian,' she said. 'Apparently he did some course on anthropology once, so the boss thought he might be useful.'

Smith held up an officious hand. 'No dogs allowed.'

'Let me look after them for you,' Archie Phillips took the leads. He'd learned to love Bear, after a disastrous first meeting, when Bear had knocked a pile of his books down a flight of stairs.

The dogs, as interested as the humans in this new activity in the river, sat obediently by Archie's feet. Jemima broke off her lecture to make a fuss of them.

Quentin Dobson, sitting on the bank, peering at the police activity, frowned. 'What's that?' he said, as one of the students waved his trowel in the air.

Libby hovered beside Gemma, wishing she was allowed in the river along with the student.

A youth in his early twenties, his straggly red hair escaping from a baseball cap, pointed to the rounded ends of two long bones, newly revealed in the mud at the side of the river. He grinned at Libby's squeak of excitement, while a dark-haired woman wearing massive, thick-soled boots waded into the water. Between them, the two researchers delicately scraped at the mud until they could retrieve both of the bones, resting them in a cardboard box.

The woman stood up and stretched. 'Well done, Rory,' she said, touching one of the bones lightly with long fingers. 'These are definitely human remains,' she added, 'most likely rib bones, but we need to take them back to the labs to date them.' She looked at Libby and Max as though suddenly noticing them. 'And you are...?'

Libby, oddly intimidated by this young but self-possessed professional woman, held out her hand. 'Libby Forest.'

The woman raised an eyebrow, wiped her hand on the back of her jeans and took Libby's hand in a firm grip. The handshake made Libby's bones crunch a little.

Libby said, 'And this is Max Ramshore.'

The younger woman narrowed her eyes, as though summing up Max. 'Charlie,' she said. 'Charlie Foxtrot.' The professional mask slipped a little and a sudden smile lit her face.

Max chuckled. 'Really?'

'My first name's Ann, actually,' she said, 'but I've been Charlie all my life. My school friends thought it funny and it stuck.'

Gemma said, 'Actually, this is Professor Foxtrot. She's been at the University for a year, now.'

Charlie waved a hand as though shrugging off her title, nodded briskly and turned back to the red-haired young man, obviously her student, asking him questions about the bones. His reply, studded with 'superior and inferior articulating regions' and 'connecting costo-vertebral joints' meant almost nothing to Libby. Charlie's replies were equally technical, so Libby stepped across to Jemima.

The elderly teacher's face glowed with the excitement of the find. 'I can't believe that after all these years, I've found something so exciting. I can't wait to find out how old these remains are.'

Charlie had overheard and turned around. 'Well done. It's quite a discovery. We'll need a few days, but my students will be thrilled to help find out everything we can.'

Max said, 'How much can you tell from these bones?'

Charlie took a moment to think, hunched, her hands tucked into the pockets of her jeans. 'Well, the skull will help a lot. Rory...' The student had gone back to his colleagues, but she beckoned him over. 'Rory can tell you what we think, so far.'

With delicate, careful movements, Rory picked up the box that held the skull. The relic lay sideways, neatly packed in cotton waste. 'It's a man,' he said. 'You see? The shape of the forehead and the big jaw.'

Libby fingered her own jaw, checking for size. The one in the box was definitely bigger. 'I see what you mean.'

'We don't have the pelvis, but we're pretty sure,' the student said. He grinned at Libby. 'The teeth are worn, which suggests the man was roughly middle-aged, but that's a guess.'

'How long has he been here?' Max asked.

'We need to do some carbon dating, using accelerator mass spectrometry. AMS for short.'

Libby tried to look intelligent. 'Does that mean you'll have to send the bones away?'

Rory's grin widened. 'It just so happens, we have a spectrometer at the university. So we can do it ourselves, although it will take a few days. If it turns out that the bones are old, maybe even hundreds of years old, it would mean the body hasn't been in the water all that time. The skeleton would have disintegrated.' He jiggled from one leg to the other, as excited as Libby. She feared he might drop the box in his excitement.

Charlie explained. 'Either someone dug him up recently and dumped him in the river, or, more likely, he was washed away from his original resting place. We had two or three days of heavy rain, a week or so ago. That would explain why there are only a few bones. Most of them must have gone down the river, out to the Bristol Channel.'

Max was squinting at the skull. 'What's that?' He pointed to the back of the skull, where there was a small hole through the bone. 'It looks as though someone hit our gentleman over the head.'

Libby, fascinated, leaned past Max, to better see the hole in the skull. 'Could that be deliberate?' she asked.

'Possibly,' Rory said. He shot a glance at Libby, his eyes shining. 'But not necessarily. We can't jump to conclusions, although I can't see any sign of healing, which would mean this might – just possibly – have been inflicted at the time of death. But that doesn't mean it's the cause of death.'

Charlie took the box from him. 'Quite right, Rory. We need to research this properly.' She flashed her sudden smile at Max. 'Gemma here tells me you two are the local experts on solving Somerset murders.' She turned back to the riverbank, 'You never know. We may have a genuine murder mystery for you. We'll all have to be patient. We get used to that, in this business.'

Just then, an angry voice shattered the excitement of the dig. For a second, Libby thought it was Chesterton Wendlebury again, and her stomach clenched. She swung round, determined not to let him intimidate her, only to find the voice belonged instead to a small, sharp-faced man wearing heavy boots and waving a hefty walking stick. He wore a substantial anorak, although the sun was already beating down and the BBC weather forecaster had talked excitedly about 'four more sunny days before the current mini heatwave breaks'. A map poked out from one pocket of the stranger's anorak. A thin woman trailed in his wake, frowning and biting her lips. Walkers. And the man meant business.

'You interfering students,' he shouted. 'Get out of our way. This part of the county is free for us to walk in and I'm not letting a bunch of lazy kids stop me going where I'm entitled.'

The man had clearly mistaken Charlie for a student and in his fury failed to notice the police tape.

Charlie turned. 'I beg your pardon?' she said, steel barely concealed beneath the words. 'If you try to disturb these bones,' she went on, 'you'll be in trouble. This is an official burial ground. I'm afraid you'll have to walk somewhere else.' She waved a hand that encompassed miles of countryside. 'There's plenty of space for everyone.'

'Why, you jumped-up—' the man stopped talking as Gemma held out her police badge.

'Detective Constable Humberstone,' she said sweetly, 'and this is a police scene.' She pointed at the bright yellow tape. 'I advise you to leave quietly without disturbing the peace any further.'

The newcomer jerked his stick at Gemma, then seemed to think better of it and turned away. 'Little Hitlers, the lot of you,' he grunted. 'And you women are the worst of all.'

His wife, a small, mousy woman, tugged at his arm. 'Leave it alone, Tom, please.'

5

CRUSTS AND CRUMBS CAFÉ

Libby arrived at the Crusts and Crumbs Café at nine thirty the next morning, her head full of plans for new recipes. As the Innovation and Development Consultant, she was responsible for new cake and chocolate recipes, and since Angela now employed more staff than had been possible in the bakery, the Café's precursor, no longer had to arrive early to bake the first batches of bread.

She parked her orange Jeep, Max's wedding present to her, just outside the kitchen. A shiver ran down her spine as she locked the car and walked the few steps to the café door. She'd been kidnapped from that same kitchen just before her wedding, and the familiar mixed feelings of terror, anger and helplessness hit her anew every time she entered the premises.

She squared her shoulders and strode inside, determined to shake off the memory of the terrifying events that took place during her most recent murder enquiry, into the death of a man found in the Avon Gorge. Once in the warmth and bustle of the busy kitchen, she relaxed as she breathed in the smells: warm bread, coffee and spices.

Mandy turned. 'Hi.' A white cap covered her black hair, which she'd pulled into a ponytail. She'd removed the rings, hoops, bars and studs from her nose, lips and ears and an apron covered her dark crimson dress. Only a slash of bright purple lipstick marked her out as a Goth as she poured cake mixture into a series of tins.

Libby sniffed the air again and pulled on gloves. 'Ginger and lemon?'

'Right as always. One of your best recipes, I think.'

To Mandy's right, Annabel Pearson balanced trays of rolls on both arms, carrying them through to the café.

Angela Miles, Libby's friend and the manager of the café, popped her head through the door. 'I thought I heard your voice,' she said. 'I'm glad you're here. Everyone in Exham seems to have "just popped in" first thing this morning, hoping to find out more about the bones at the abbey. Why don't you come through and serve, and put a few folk out of their misery?'

Libby hesitated. 'I was planning to spend all day on chocolates. I wanted to try a new filling – peanut butter and strawberry.'

Angela made a face. 'Are you sure? I can't quite...'

Libby relented. 'Maybe it can wait. I do believe you're as keen to hear all the details as everyone else.'

'Naturally,' Angela said. 'This place thrives on gossip. Come through, and you'll see.'

'You're the boss.'

Heads turned as Libby entered and the hum of voices paused momentarily, before starting up again, more loudly.

Angela was right. The café was already heaving with customers. Every plate groaned with chocolate cake, Victoria sponge or Black Forest Gateau and a line of customers chattered like sparrows as they queued for sandwiches to take onto the beach.

Libby served sausage rolls and cheese baps to hungry workers from the half-dozen estate agents on the High Street and fielded their questions.

'Now, do tell, Mrs Forest,' said Peter, one of the young men working in the local estate agency, taking possession of a tuna sandwich and a slice of cake. His waistline seemed to grow by inches every year. 'Mrs Miles told us about finding the bones, but I bet you have all the gory details, seeing as you're in the pocket of the police.' There was an edge to his voice.

'I don't know much,' Libby said equably, ignoring the jibe. 'But the bones look very old.'

'So, no one for you to put in prison.'

Libby started at the sudden spite in Peter's voice, but said, smoothly, 'I don't think we're looking for any present-day suspects.'

Several heads jerked up.

Libby bit her lip. She'd given away more than she'd intended.

Annabel said, 'Suspects? You mean, the person was murdered?'

Libby waved a hand in the air, trying to retrieve the situation. 'Oh, no. Not at all. There's just a bit of damage to the skull, that's all.'

The chatter in the café, which had lessened while the customers listened, started up again with renewed vigour.

'I suppose,' Annabel said, thoughtfully, 'the bones are likely to belong to a monk, since they were found just outside the abbey.'

Libby shook her head. 'We really don't know at the moment. But it's possible.'

'But there haven't been monks there since the sixteenth century.' Annabel's eyes looked as though they'd grown stalks. 'So, the skeleton must be four hundred years old.' She took a clean plate from the rack and nudged a scone delicately into its centre. 'A Tudor murder – how exciting.'

'But it might not be a murder...'

Annabel had already moved off.

Libby gave up and retreated to the kitchen, the clamour in the café even louder now.

'Well,' said Angela. 'If you were hoping to calm things down, you've failed, miserably.'

Libby started work on her new chocolate recipes. She'd leave the customers to make up their own stories about the bones in the river.

6

While Libby was at the café, Charlie rang Max. 'Do you have time to come over to the university this afternoon? We've been working on the bones this morning and I'd like to tell you what we've discovered.'

He chuckled. Libby would have loved to accompany him and she was going to be green with envy that he'd found out more about the mystery man in the river. Still, he wasn't going to turn down the invitation.

Bear and Shipley looked at him with pleading eyes, but he hardened his heart. Wasn't the room where the man's bones were stored some kind of special, germ-free environment? Dogs were unlikely to be welcome.

'Sorry, boys. I'll take you out when I get home. Play nicely.' He grinned. He'd be better directing that remark to Fuzzy, whose favourite activity apart from sleeping in the sun was sitting on the banister at the top of the stairs, out of reach of Shipley, swishing her tail.

He filled the water bowls and left the house.

As the sun shone, already high in the sky and secure under

the influence of a spell of high pressure, caused by 'something to do with the jet stream', as Libby had said over breakfast, Max drove to Bristol. He grinned to himself. Libby pretended to be puzzled by so much, while in fact she was sharply intelligent. She just liked to hide it – an approach that had worked well in the past with people like Jemima who enjoyed showing off their knowledge. Max preferred to take a more direct approach. He was looking forward to talking to Charlie and finding out how much she'd learned about their skeleton.

The sunshine hit him as he opened the door of the car. It seemed to bounce off the concrete of the car park. For once, he'd needed the air conditioning in the car more than the heater, and the wall of heat took him by surprise. He'd never get used to the joy of a glorious June day.

He made his way towards the plain brick building containing the physics department of the university as Charlie appeared at a window, waving madly.

She greeted him at the door. 'Come in, I've been longing to tell you all about this man.'

She ushered him through a small tea room, and he shrugged into the white coat she held for him, pulled on white gloves and followed her into the cool, light room where the skeletal remains lay.

The skull looked stark and lonely on the bench, its empty eye-sockets pointed at the ceiling. One side of the jaw was broken and the hole in the side of the head looked, to Max's amateur eyes, to be about the size of a large stick.

Charlie stood beside him and pointed. 'As we said at the dig, it's an adult male. The size of the jaw and the forehead – I'll keep to layman's language unless you want the full science? I'll be writing a report when we have all the information.'

Max held up a defensive hand. 'Please, keep it simple. I'm

most interested in whether or not the man could have been a monk from Cleeve Abbey – how exciting would that be? Of course, he could be a farmer, or a carter or something, but everything about monks fascinates me – how could they bear to live as they did, never seeing anyone outside? Cleeve Abbey's in a wonderful, quiet spot, but I'd hate to be cut off from the world. I gather the monks weren't even allowed to talk to each other.'

Charlie smiled. 'Well, this was a Cistercian monastery, which means it was strict, but people are expert at getting around the rules – the monks used sign language to communicate in silence. But I'm afraid we're getting ahead of ourselves. At the moment, we don't know what our man did for a living, or how long ago he died. His position in the river beside the ruins, near the monks' burial area, suggests he may have come from the abbey. He could easily have been washed out of the graveyard there. But it's only circumstantial evidence, remember.'

Max knew his disappointment showed on his face.

Charlie laughed. 'On the other hand, we've learned a few facts. From the skull we have here, and these two other bones, one of which is the femur—'

'The thigh bone?' Max said.

'Exactly, and the third bone is from the palm of the hand.' She pointed to another, smaller, bone. 'The third metacarpal. It runs from the wrist to the middle finger.' She showed him on her own hand and then pointed to the skeleton that stood in one corner of the room. 'There, you can see it clearly.'

Max wiggled his own finger, watching the movement of his palm, fascinated in spite of himself. As he was thinking through the information, wishing he'd concentrated more in biology at school, Rory, Charlie's student, bounced into the room.

Charlie glanced his way. 'Hi, I thought you were going home?

The exams finished last week. I was surprised you were still here for the dig, yesterday.'

Rory grinned. 'Had a bit of a party last night.' He winced.

'Hangover?' Max suggested.

Rory shoved his baseball cap farther back on his head, leaving spikes of red hair standing up above his forehead. 'I was going to move out today, but who'd want to miss a real-life mystery? Not me.'

'Well, why don't you tell Max what we've discovered about this man?' Charlie said. 'I've explained that it will take a few days to date his bones.'

Rory nodded, his face pink with excitement.

Max said, 'I'm hoping he's a medieval or Tudor monk from the abbey.'

Rory nodded, solemnly, and before Max's eyes, seemed to morph into a teacher, one finger pointing to the bones, the other stroking his chin. 'The bones tell us a great deal,' he said. 'The thigh bone is useful for measurement as we can estimate the owner's height.'

Max kept a grave face, defying the urge to laugh at the student's wrinkled brow and intense expression. Rory looked as though he were struggling to remember the contents of a textbook.

Rory, oblivious, carried on. 'That gives us a clue as to nutrition. Only an estimate, of course. We don't have enough of this body to be sure, but so far as we can give an educated guess, this man's about five foot ten inches tall.' He flashed a grin at Max, relaxing. 'That's tallish for a medieval or Tudor monk but not out of the question. This guy had a decent lifestyle, with plenty to eat and drink. Poor people tended to be shorter.'

'Can you tell his age?' Max asked, impressed. The lad certainly knew his stuff.

'I'm so glad you asked that,' Charlie put in. 'We can gauge it fairly accurately. You see, every skull consists of different bones, and in a newborn baby there are gaps called fontanels between the bones.'

'I remember my children had soft patches at the top of the skull,' Max said.

Charlie nodded. 'That's right. Scary to a new parent, but actually quite safe.' She turned to Rory. 'Can you explain what the soft patches are for?'

Rory was back in textbook mode. 'The fontanels allow movement between the bones during birth, so the baby's head can pass through the birth canal.'

Max winced.

Charlie laughed. 'Quite. The bones gradually fuse together, mostly during the first two years of life. Rory?' she pointed to a set of zigzag lines on the skull.

'Those are sutures,' he said. 'Complete fusion of the joints between the bones continues over life and allows us to estimate age – although, it's not exact. But, given the state of fusion here, we think this man was between thirty and thirty-five years of age.'

'Wow.' For a moment, Max was stunned. Suddenly, the bones were no longer anonymous. They belonged to someone roughly the same height and age as Max's own son, Joe.

'Yes,' Rory's eyes were on his face. 'It brings him alive, doesn't it? Makes him human. But there's something else we found that will blow your mind.'

'Go on, then. I'm ready.'

Rory said, triumphantly, 'This man was a clerk, working on medieval manuscripts.'

Max blinked. 'How can you possibly know that?'

'I told you you'd be surprised. Look at his teeth. Here's one, the canine on the right side.' Rory was jiggling on the spot, unable to contain his excitement.

Max leaned and looked, but it was just an old, yellowy tooth. He looked again. There was a hint, just a speck, of something in the gap between the canine and the next tooth. 'Is that blue paint?' he asked, feeling foolish.

Rory punched the air. 'Yay! You got it.'

Max looked from him to Charlie.

'Well done,' she said. 'We investigated a fragment of that blueness, and it turns out it's lapis lazuli. That's a mineral pigment used in illuminating manuscripts. It's also used in jewellery and inlaid in boxes and so on, so it's not just monks who used it, but given where this man was found, I think we can answer your question. He was most probably a monk, living at the abbey at least four hundred years ago. What's more, he was one of the scribes, which means he was something of an intellectual with at least a rudimentary knowledge of Latin, copying and illustrating sacred texts.'

'So, he really was a monk, living at Cleeve Abbey?' Max said. 'I'm flabbergasted.' He frowned. 'And, you've been teasing me, pretending you didn't know.'

She was laughing. 'I'm sorry, I couldn't resist stringing you along a little. That young Detective Constable Humberstone kept singing your praises as an investigator, and I thought I'd try to impress you. To be honest, we only worked out our monk's profession because Rory read about a recent similar discovery at the University of York. I bet our monk used to lick his paintbrush. You can imagine him, can't you, bent over a manuscript, drawing a line of blue and putting the brush in his mouth? Just like a child in school, sucking a biro.' She turned to Rory. 'I'm gasping and the coffee pot's empty next door. Could you nip out and get us some more? And maybe some water.'

As he left, she winked at Max. 'I'm going to get at least one paper out of this – which is just as well. I have to turn in a regular stream of articles to academic journals in order to keep my position at the university and I was running dry.'

Max said, 'I suppose you can't tell me whether or not our monk was murdered.'

'Not yet,' she said, 'but that's a very interesting hole in his skull. Between you and me, I wouldn't be at all surprised.'

7

SHERRY

Max could hardly wait to tell Libby about his trip to the university. He'd phoned to tell her he'd be in Bristol that afternoon and she'd been furious to have missed it. But when he arrived home, she was still out. 'Long day in the café, I suppose. Hordes of summer visitors,' he told Bear, as he fed the dogs, jingled their leads and took them out for a run in the fields, enjoying the soft evening air.

Returning to a still-empty house, he clattered around the kitchen, making himself a quick meal of pasta with a pile of grated cheese on top. He was quite alone, apart from the animals. He could count on one hand the number of times that had happened since their wedding.

Grunting, knowing he sounded like the old fogey his son Joe called him, he piled his food onto a tray and took it into the study.

He turned on the television for company and flicked idly through the channels, muttering that it had been easier before all these cable channels were set up, when there was less choice and you watched what happened to be on.

Bear looked at him with liquid, sympathetic eyes.

'Come on up, then.'

Bear heaved himself onto the settee, his head in Max's lap, while Shipley curled up at his feet. Finding nothing he wanted to watch, he hit the mute button, feeling slightly less lonely with the soundless, moving picture for company.

That was when he saw the note, tucked half-under an old book. His heart lurched as he went over and picked up the scrap of paper. Libby had been kidnapped from the café, just before Christmas, and a note had been left for Max. Panic gripped him for a split second. Was history repeating itself?

His heartbeat slowed as he unfolded the piece of paper. This was no ransom note. It was in Libby's writing – almost impossible to read. She must have come back home while he was out. He did his best to decipher the words. It was written in Libby's signature chatty style, as though she was talking to him.

Sorry, I'll be out this evening at Jemima's hound.

'Hound?' Bear jumped down from the sofa at the exclamation and loped across to Max's side.

Max rolled his eyes. 'I suppose she means, "house". Such dreadful writing.'

The note went on:

Dr Phillips was working today, although shouldn't he have retired from the library by now? He must be at least seventy. He's bringing books for me to see and Jemima asked for the dogs to come too. If you're not exhausted from playing with bones and the gorgeous Charlie, why don't you come and bring them? Eat first. There's some cold salmon, a special

*salad and some of the dressing you like in the fridge. Love
Libby. PS (Libby loved a PS) Quentin's coming too – a thong
triangle?*

It took a moment for Max to register that she wasn't referring
to Jemima's underwear, but to 'a love triangle'.

Wells, where Jemima lived, was less than twenty miles away.
Max took his rapidly cooling pasta back to the kitchen and
scraped the plate into the compost bin, wishing he'd read Libby's
note before preparing his own dull meal, or had at least noticed
the salad in the fridge.

He called the dogs. 'Sorry,' he said to Fuzzy, who'd followed
him into the kitchen, sniffing the air. 'We're leaving you again.
Have some of Libby's best salmon, but don't tell her I gave it to
you.'

* * *

Perched on a hard chair at Jemima's dining table, Libby sipped a
glass of sweet sherry and surreptitiously glanced at her watch.
When would Max get here?

Archie Phillips flicked through a pile of books and papers,
following a complicated trail of yellow Post-it notes. Quentin
Dobson kept himself busy refilling glasses, while Jemima
Bakewell leaned on her elbows, looking from one to the other of
her male suitors, beaming.

Libby pointed to a photo on the mantelpiece. It showed
Jemima surrounded by a group of laughing women wearing
sensible shoes and sunhats. 'Greece?' Libby suggested.

'A holiday with old friends from my teaching days.' Jemima
sighed. 'Happy times.'

'But not as exciting as finding ancient bones,' Quentin said, refilling her glass.

Archie, vague and mild-mannered, glanced up from one of his books, *Somerset Myths and Legends*. His eyes gleamed under bushy eyebrows.

The rivalry between the two men hung heavy in the air.

At long last, when Libby felt she could not manage a single sip more of the cloying sherry, Max arrived with the dogs.

'So glad you could come,' Jemima said. 'This is all terribly exciting. Dr Phillips has brought some books that might help with the history of the bones.'

'Do call me Archie, Max. I feel quite old enough already. And, you've arrived at exactly the right moment. I've found the passage I wanted to show you and Libby.'

Max smiled. 'Before we get into your books, if you'll forgive me, Archie, I must update you on the information Charlie Foxtrot at the university gave me about those bones.'

For a moment he paused.

'Go on, then,' Libby said. 'Stop milking it.'

Max told them about the lapis lazuli. 'Although we don't have a definite age to the bones, it's looking very likely they belong to a medieval monk. And, given where you found them, Jemima,' their hostess blushed with pleasure, 'I think we can assume this monk came from Cleeve Abbey. Which is what we were all hoping, of course.'

Libby said, 'That's such good news. I'd far rather investigate an ancient death than a recent one.'

Jemima said, 'Fascinating. Knowing the man's occupation brings him to life. In fact, don't you think we should give him a name?'

'Excellent idea,' Archie said. 'How about Benedict?'

'Let's not confuse our lowly monk with the founder of the monastic tradition,' Quentin countered.

'Not that lowly,' Max pointed out. 'He probably didn't do much in the way of manual labour if he was one of the illuminators. How about Bernie? That sounds suitably monkish.'

Quentin leaned over to Bear and muttered something Libby didn't quite catch in the dog's ear. It sounded a little like, 'Idiot.'

Archie raised a bushy eyebrow. 'I'm afraid monks didn't use diminutives in quite the same way we do nowadays.'

Libby tried not to fidget as the argument dragged on. Justin, Jocelyn and Julian were all rejected. If they weren't too modern, they were too feminine.

Finally, Jemima suggested, 'Bernard.'

Silence fell. Libby held her breath.

No one objected.

'Good idea,' Quentin said. 'The perfect name for a medieval monk. Well done.'

Jemima blushed again. She was having the time of her life and Libby hid a smile. Jemima was bound to have her way, if Quentin and Archie had anything to do with it.

'Now,' Archie said, opening a green, leather-backed book. 'I've been gathering information on Cleeve Abbey, to see if there is any evidence our mystery man lived there.'

The others squinted sideways to read the titles on the spine.

'This,' Archie went on, 'is a translation of Pope Gregory's written Rules of St Benedict – that is, the rules the monasteries were founded upon and that the Cistercian monks at Cleeve Abbey would have obeyed.'

Libby nodded, seriously, wishing she knew more about monasteries than her schoolgirl knowledge that they had suffered under Henry VIII.

Archie looked, eyebrows raised, at Max, who nodded.

'Bernard lived in the sixteenth century, according to Charlie Foxtrot.'

'About the time of the dissolution of the monasteries,' Quentin said loudly, as though concerned his voice hadn't been heard for a while.

Archie nodded. A smile played around his lips, as though he had something up his sleeve, and was about to release his bombshell.

Max had noticed it, too. 'Go on, Archie. We can see you're bursting to tell us the news.'

Archie glanced around, checking everyone was listening. Satisfied, he slid a thin booklet from between the pages of the book. 'I discovered this in Wells Cathedral Library. It's a copy of a letter sent to the king's receiver, begging for the monastery at Cleeve to be saved from the suppression – which was another word for the dissolution of the monasteries. But it failed, for the land was leased to private individuals, leaving thirteen monks homeless.'

'That's so sad,' Libby said. 'What did they do?'

Archie replied, 'We know what happened to some of them. Half a dozen went to another, larger, monastery until that one was also suppressed, but there are several others of which there are no records.'

Jemima's face had fallen. 'So, we don't know what happened to our Bernard. Was he destitute after the place closed, or did he get a job somewhere?'

Archie gestured at his piles of documents. 'I've spent all day trying to find out what happened to the Cleeve Abbey monks, but with no success. I'm afraid we will have to look elsewhere for answers.'

Max opened his mouth and closed it again.

'What is it?' Libby asked.

He sighed. 'I can hardly believe I'm saying this, but maybe we should see if the History Society members can help.'

'Funny you should say that,' Libby said. 'We're meeting in a few days, and judging by the excitement at the café today, everyone in the society will be there.'

Libby was right. The next regular meeting of the Exham-on-Sea History Society was almost as packed as the café had been.

Marjorie and William Halfstead were there, as always, as were Annabel Pearson and Joanna Sheffield. Archie, Jemima and Quentin sat in a row on Angela's pale sofa, like the three wise monkeys, Jemima in the middle, her cheeks pink with pleasure. Perhaps, leading her quiet life, buried in history and her school, she'd never been waited upon hand and foot by two eligible widowers. If so, Libby decided, she deserved her small triumphs.

'Now then.' The angry walker from the dig site cut across the hum of conversation. 'I'm a busy man, I am. I'm told you lot are the local experts on Somerset history, so when do we hear about this skeleton?'

Angela smiled, the perfect hostess. 'You're very welcome to our group, Mr Reeves, and you're quite right, we have several experts here. Dr Phillips,' she indicated Archie, 'is the librarian at Wells Cathedral, and certainly an expert. As is Quentin Dobson from the museum in Watchet and also Jemima Bakewell, who's treatise on a comparison between the Iron Age in Britain and the later Roman civilisation was very well received in archaeological circles.'

Jemima's cheeks glowed scarlet with delight. Libby marvelled at Angela's tact.

'But the rest of us, of course, are interested amateurs,' Angela continued.

'Aye, well, that's as may be,' said the man, less belligerently. 'And you can call me Tom, if we're all on first-name terms here. I expect you're all wondering how I know about this group.'

Marjorie Halfstead nodded, uncertainly. No one had ever gate-crashed the society in quite this way.

'Well, I care about Somerset, lived here all my life, like to know what's what. I got talking to that policeman at the dig. Fine fellow. Knows a thing or two.'

Libby and Angela exchanged glances.

'PC Ian Smith?' Angela ventured.

'That's him. He told me about this group, and said I should call in at the café to find out more. I gather it's the hub of life in this town.' He nodded at Angela. 'So I did, saw your poster on the wall and here I am.'

'And your two friends?' Angela's smile was warm.

'My good wife, Winifred, and her sister, Rosalind Barnstaple.'

The two women shared similar beaky noses that jutted out starkly and marked them as sisters. Otherwise, they looked very different.

Winifred was thin with the kind of saggy skin that hints at rapid weight loss. Her light, sandy hair was turning grey, and she wore a drab khaki dress, several sizes too big, under a brown cardigan.

Rosalind, in contrast, boasted a head of abundant hair, its vibrant red rather obviously from a bottle. It was caught up on top of her head in an oversized multicoloured clasp. Her silk, sleeveless dress swished elegantly as she rose to smile around the room as though acknowledging an audience.

Libby said, 'You're all interested in local history?'

Rosalind returned to her chair. 'Indeed we are.'

Tom interrupted. 'Aye, well, the ladies are. If you ask me, there's too much half-baked history around here. What with Glastonbury and Druids and whatnot.' He leaned forward, his hands on his knees, and screwed up his turkey-cock face in disgust. 'It's all a lot of tosh.'

Quentin Dobson half-rose. 'I say—' he began, but Tom Reeves ignored him and said,

'But, if this skeleton find can stop that Wendlebury character ruining the countryside, I don't mind hearing more about it.'

Quentin subsided.

Libby frowned. What did he mean? Was Chesterton Wendlebury up to something? Before she could ask, Archie confronted the newcomer.

'I can assure you, the history we discuss is not nonsense. We have a most interesting past in this part of the world, as you suggest, and I'd thank you to be respectful.' He settled his spectacles more securely on his nose. 'Do I take it you have academic credentials?'

Tom Reeves snorted. 'Not me. Don't need 'em. Too busy earning a living for book learning and all these universities. I leave all that to the younger generation – a bunch of snowflakes, if you ask me. I'm a plain-talking farmer, that's what I am. I've been farming in Somerset all my life, and my father and grandfather before me.' He jabbed a finger in Archie's direction. 'I learned my business in the university of life. That's where I get my,' he snorted, 'credentials, as you call them.'

Angela cleared her throat. 'Before we go any further, let's all have another cup of coffee. And Tom and Winfred and – er –

Rosalind, why don't you try some of Libby's lemon cake. She very generously provides it for our meetings.'

Winifred said, in a voice so quiet Libby had to lean forward to hear it, 'That will be lovely. Won't it, Tom?'

'Aye, well.' With a final scornful glare at Archie, Tom folded his arms. 'I don't mind a slice of cake. Looks OK.'

Under cover of a general move by the regular members of the society to help themselves to cake and smooth over Tom Reeves' rudeness, Angela murmured in Libby's ear, 'I think that's meant to be a compliment. Shall I tell him about the cookery books you've written?'

Libby, fighting wild laughter, shook her head. 'He's very, um, aggressive, isn't he?'

Angela said, 'He's got some sort of an axe to grind about new homes in Somerset and he wants us to join him in objecting to any more.'

'Well, there have been plenty of grumbles in the local paper about building in the countryside: expensive homes for second home owners that local people can't afford. Do you think Tom wants to stage protests with placards and things at County Hall? That might be fun. But what does that have to do with Chesterton Wendlebury?'

She was interrupted by a sudden cry of surprise. Marjorie exclaimed, 'Rosalind Barnstaple. I knew I'd heard your name. You're from that TV programme. The one about ghosts.'

Rosalind Barnstaple bowed her head in acknowledgement. Strands of her auburn hair had escaped from their clasp to curl like wire springs around her face. She'd been almost unnoticed as Tom Reeves took centre stage, but now she seized the moment, rose to her feet once more and looked around the room. 'I'm sorry we invited ourselves so unexpectedly,' she said. Her voice was high-pitched and carried traces of cut-glass vowels. Rosalind smiled at Angela. 'I'm especially grateful to Mrs Miles for inviting us into her lovely home. You see,' she continued, suddenly animated, 'I'm very excited to hear about this body at Cleeve Abbey. I've been looking for somewhere to conduct one of my investigations into the supernatural and I think Cleeve will be perfect for my purposes.'

Libby said, 'But there are just a few bones at the moment. We don't know much about it until we hear more from Bristol University, where they're using something called a... called a...' she struggled to remember the name.

Rosalind smiled. 'Accelerator mass spectrometry? AMS for short. Yes, I know the machine. And, it will tell us how old the bones are, and give us information about what happened to the physical person who lived in the body, but, quite frankly, I'm not so interested in mere facts. Facts get in the way of understanding.' As she spoke, her voice rose. Finally, she exclaimed, dramatically, 'I care about souls.'

Someone in the room stifled a laugh.

Libby swallowed. 'Do you mean, seances?'

Rosalind smiled with a touch of condescension. 'Oh, I'm not a medium. I'm a paranormal scientist.'

Just as well. Libby breathed more easily. She'd once crossed paths with a group called the Pathway, who scammed newly bereaved relatives by pretending to speak to them in the afterlife. She would have nothing to do with any more seances.

'I can see you're anxious,' Rosalind said, returning to her seat and graciously accepting a slice of cake. 'There's nothing to fear. All I want to do is spend a little time in the abbey, drinking in the atmosphere, watching and listening.'

'Well, that's easy enough,' Marjorie said. 'Anyone can go to the abbey. It's open to the public. We were there having a picnic when Jemima found the bones.'

'Oh, my dear, you don't understand,' said Rosalind, with a trill of laughter. 'I don't mean any old daytime visit to the ruins. I prefer to spend the night in ancient buildings, for my research into paranormal phenomena. I've been all over the country, you know, and Somerset has one of the richest collections of possible sites for psychic manifestations.'

'Do you mean you're going ghost-hunting?' Angela asked.

'Exactly.'

Marjorie shivered, 'In the dark?'

'Quite. I have permission from the authorities for a research session at Cleeve Abbey and I'd like a few members of this society to come with me. Who's brave enough?'

'Well,' said Libby. 'You can count me out.'

EXHAM HOUSE

'I almost wish I'd been there,' Max said, as Libby recounted the meeting, later that night. He avoided the History Society whenever possible, finding the chatter tiring. He preferred to spend the evening using his computer to uncover financial fraud, or investigate the growing spate of animal thefts, on behalf of clients.

'You know you hate gossip, but you would have enjoyed this.' She was curled into an immense brown leather chair in Max's study, with Bear lying at her feet, alternately grunting and passing wind. Libby fanned her hand in front of her face. 'What on earth did you feed Bear this evening?'

'Liver. Lightly broiled.' He licked his lips, in a bad imitation of Anthony Hopkins.

'Thank you, Hannibal,' Libby said, 'but I don't think your future lies in acting. Anyway, I said I won't go on this ridiculous ghost-hunting expedition. I don't want anything to do with supernatural hocus-pocus.'

'Mm,' said Max. 'Sounds like fun, to me. I mean, if plenty of people are there, there's nothing to be scared of.'

'I'm not scared,' Libby objected. 'At least, not very. Although I admit I'm easily spooked, especially in the dark.'

Bear stood up, sighed, turned round and lay down once more across Libby's feet.

She said, 'Have you ever had that thing where you look in the mirror at night, and expect to see a ghost or an axe-murderer behind your back? It's terrifying.'

Max groaned. 'I haven't, but I will now, I'm sure. Thank you for that thought.' He put on a wheedling voice, 'I think we should go along with this search for the supernatural at the abbey. We could take the dogs with us. They'll keep us safe.'

Libby looked hard at her husband. It was the first time he'd shown real interest in the History Society so she wanted to encourage him. 'Well, I wouldn't want to go without you, but I'm not sure about taking the dogs. I think they might upset Rosalind. She has very strong views and Shipley at least might be too – what shall I say – exuberant. And Bear doesn't like ghosts any more than I do. Do you remember, at one time he wouldn't come into your drawing room at all, and we thought there was a ghost here.'

'But he got over it. I reckon he just found it cold. It's been much cosier since I put the wood burner in, although now, of course, we shouldn't be burning wood at all.'

'I know. Things change so fast, don't they? At least we don't need to burn anything at the moment to keep warm. This weather's so lovely. In fact, it's almost too hot at times. Maybe we should think about air conditioning indoors.'

'Or we could just open the windows and save ourselves a small fortune,' Max said. 'But to get back to this outing at the abbey.' He went to his desk and collected an armful of books, flopping back on the sofa under their weight. 'I looked these out. You probably remember my old book *Myths and Legends of the*

West Country and I've got a few others. I've even found this old pamphlet.' He waved a thin, tattered volume in the air. 'I've no idea where it came from, but it was written in the 1950s, by someone who used to live at the abbey when part of it was divided into flats.'

Libby, excited, heaved Bear from her feet and climbed onto the sofa next to Max. She leaned over as he opened the pamphlet. 'What a wonderful name. Cleeva Clapp. You couldn't make it up.'

'Actually, someone did – her parents, who were caretakers at the abbey. They loved the place so much they called her Cleevena, and she very sensibly shortened it to Cleeva. I don't think they were to blame for the "Clapp" part.'

'Poor woman,' Libby sympathised. 'Anyway, what does she say?'

'Well, along with plenty of information about Henry VIII's dissolution of the monasteries, which I'm sure Jemima and Archie will use to keep us amused if we go ghost-hunting, she talks about the "back in the ages feeling" in the ruins. And she says it's only haunted by the "the good" there.'

Libby touched the brown, slightly musty-smelling pamphlet. 'This is fascinating. Look, it cost sixpence when it was published.' She spotted the twinkle in Max's eyes. 'You really want to go on this midnight vigil affair, don't you?'

Max had the grace to look shifty. 'There's one more thing I didn't tell you about. Do you remember my American colleague, Reg? He came here, about the time of that murder at Wells Cathedral.'

Libby clasped her hands against her chest. 'How could I forget? He's gorgeous. If it hadn't been for Mandy, I'd have swooned all over him while he was here. But she got there first, and Reg seemed just as taken with her as she was with him. Not that their affair lasted long, of course. I suppose Reg is a bit too old for her. She was going through a bit of a bad patch with Steve, but they soon got back together. In fact, I'm not sure that Steve knew anything about Reg. He'd gone to study music in London at the time, which was, of course, part of the reason they'd quarrelled.'

'Well, Reg is back in the country, and still focused on finding stolen valuable books.'

Libby cheered. 'He's here, in England?'

'For a few weeks, and turning heads everywhere he goes.'

'That's not surprising. He's about six foot seven and looks exactly like Michael Jordan.'

'And, if you remember, he'd come for dinner that evening when Bear was behaving so oddly, and we discovered there had been a murder here, centuries ago, at the time of the Battle of Sedgemoor.'

'You're right. And he was so excited, hoping you had ghosts here. Just as well you discovered it was all down to poor heating.' She thought for a moment. 'I suppose Rosalind's right. There are plenty of historic places in Somerset that are ripe for psychic investigation. Do you think Reg will want to come to the abbey?'

'I'll give him a buzz. When he hears, I won't be able to keep him away,' Max said. 'He's always wishing he could meet a real British ghost.' He rubbed his hands together, ignoring Libby's sigh. 'I think you'll find this night-time expedition is going to be fun.'

Mandy stood at the kitchen window of Hope Cottage on Saturday, waiting for Libby to drive up. As the sole tenant since Libby's marriage, Mandy felt stupidly nervous whenever her landlady, and employer in the cake and chocolates business, visited. The responsibility of keeping Hope Cottage clean and tidy had descended on Mandy's shoulders, and she didn't want to let Libby down.

Today, with some news she wanted to share, she'd invited both Libby and Max to lunch. Steve, her boyfriend, would be here as well. She'd insisted on that.

She swallowed, beset by second thoughts. Maybe it hadn't been such a good idea, after all, to invite Libby to her own house. She'd hosted so many lunches and dinners here. What made Mandy think she could compete?

Then, Libby's orange Jeep appeared and screeched to a halt. Mandy relaxed a little. Her boss was a terrible driver.

Steve called from the living room. 'Sounds like Libby's driving?'

'She's here, and Max as well.'

Steve grunted. Mandy had always suspected he was scared of Max, and today, he was as nervous as she was. He'd even dressed in smart trousers and a shirt with a collar, although, to Mandy's relief, he'd not added a tie. She wore her favourite long dress, and net sleeves covered in pretend tattoos – she was too scared of needles to have real tats. 'Fakes mean I can change them when I like,' was her official excuse.

Libby and Max climbed out of the car and let the dogs scramble out.

Mandy flung open the front door to greet them, but they were standing with their backs turned to her. They seemed to be gazing at the lamp post.

'What on earth are you looking at, Mrs F?' Mandy shouted.

Libby turned and laughed, looking sheepish. 'Memory Lane,' she said. 'That's the lamp post I reversed my Citroen into the day I met Max. Look, you can still see the dent.'

'About time the council repainted the lamp post, then,' Mandy scoffed. 'Are you coming in, or are you going to stare at your romantic lamp post all day?'

Steve arrived at the door behind her, fidgeting nervously.

Max said, 'Good to see you, Steve. In your last year at the Royal College of Music, your aunt Angela tells me.'

Steve flushed to the roots of his hair, but Mandy beamed with pride. 'He got a first for his saxophone performance in his finals. Some weird contemporary piece, all leaps up and down the scale, but it sounded pretty good, to be fair. I enjoyed it. Sort of. And, he's all done, now. He just needs a job.'

Libby looked from one to the other. 'Congratulations, Steve. It seems only yesterday you were at Wells Cathedral School—'

'And you caught Mandy and me smoking spliffs while Mum was out.'

The ice broken, Mandy led the way into the tiny dining room, where her nerves returned. 'It's a bit messy, I'm afraid.'

Max roared with laughter. 'Don't worry. You know no one does messy like Libby. It's one of the things I love about her because she doesn't follow me around tidying up and she lets me put my feet up on the coffee table. It's a big relief, I can tell you. I thought I'd have to change my sloppy ways when we married.'

Libby sniffed the air. 'Mandy, I can smell something wonderful. Garlic?'

'I made Chicken and Chips the way you taught me when I first moved in. With your special sauce.'

Max rubbed his stomach. 'Mushrooms, garlic and brandy. One of my favourite meals.'

'He means, yet another of his favourite meals,' Libby said.

'In that case, shall we eat?'

Max, Libby and Steve settled round the table while Mandy fiddled in the kitchen. She loved cooking in the gleaming state-of-the-art kitchen Libby had installed when she first came to Exham. She'd baked her first signature cakes here – the ones that founded her reputation as the town's best baker. Mandy kept every inch of it spotless.

Proudly, she carried heaped dishes of fragrant food to the table and the friends served themselves.

'How's Sarah?' Mandy asked. Libby's son Robert and his wife were expecting their first baby in a few weeks. 'You need to get a rocking chair before the baby comes, so you can knit bootees like a proper granny.'

Libby shook her head. 'Oh, no. You saw the squares I tried to knit that time we yarn-bombed Wells. They looked like Edam cheese, where I'd dropped stitches. I'm leaving my daughter to help with the baby clothes. Ali's so different to me. She's…' Libby waved her hands in the air. 'Creative, I suppose. She designs things and makes them; you know, knitting and sewing and all those practical skills I don't have. You should see the little blanket she's crocheted.'

The others were all laughing. 'What did I say?'

Max said, 'You don't think designing cakes and chocolates that disappear from the shelves like snow in July counts as creative.'

'I never thought of it like that.'

Mandy said, 'Will Ali still be here when the baby comes?'

Libby clasped her head in mock despair and groaned. 'I really don't know. She has a place at medical school in Brazil for next January so I'm hoping she'll stay in England for the rest of this year. Andy, her boyfriend, pops back across the Atlantic from time to time; in fact he'll be back here in a few days, but he can't do that often because it costs a fortune. I know Ali misses him and I wouldn't be surprised if she disappeared to the other side of the world at any moment. You know Ali.'

Mandy shot a questioning glance at Steve. He gave a brief shake of his head, as though he didn't think it was the moment for their news, but as Mandy looked away, she intercepted a quick glance from Max. He looked from her to Steve and back, eyebrow raised. Had he guessed the reason for today's lunch, and if so, would he be supportive? Mandy couldn't tell.

He gave a short nod with a half-smile as they tucked into the food, tactfully turning the conversation to Cleeve Abbey and the likelihood of seeing a ghost.

Mandy tried to relax, breathe slowly, telling herself she was getting worked up over nothing, but the tight feeling in her chest disagreed.

11

NEWS

Max cleared every scrap of cream from his dish of strawberries and cream, finally pushing it away with a contented sigh, and leaned back in his chair. Mandy's nerves twitched.

'Your food was wonderful,' Max said. 'Especially the chicken. You're a worthy successor to Libby in that kitchen, Mandy.' His eyes met hers. 'And now that we've finished talking about babies and agreed we'll all go along to this ridiculous ghost-hunting expedition, why don't you tell us the real reason you invited us here?'

Mandy gulped. Both Libby and Max were watching, transfixed, as she took a steadying breath. 'Steve's going to stay in London, now he's finished studying. There's more work there. He's hoping to pick up some gigs, playing backing music in some of the studios, maybe start a band with some colleagues and do a bit of freelance teaching. The thing is...' her voice wavered and faded away.

She turned to Steve for support. 'Go on,' he said, 'tell them.'

A sudden lump stuck in her throat. She coughed and the words came out in a rush. 'I'm planning to go to London with him. We're getting a flat.' Tears prickled her eyes. What would Libby think? She'd been so kind, training Mandy through her apprenticeship and letting her live at Hope Cottage for a ridiculously low rent. Would she feel betrayed? Who would take over as her right-hand woman, making all the recipes she'd developed over the past few years, finding new sales outlets and flirting with buyers over the phone? Mandy felt like a traitor. She gave a little hiccup. 'I'm very sorry.'

With a shout of delight, Libby pushed herself away from the table and ran to throw her arms around Mandy. 'You idiot, there's no need to be sorry. It's great news. Of course you want to be with Steve – you've been together for long enough to know your own minds – and London is the most exciting place in the world for young people. You'll have a ball. Congratulations to both of you.'

Max stood to shake Steve's hand, and Mandy could hold back her tears no longer. 'I'll miss you.' She sniffed, scrubbing at her nose with a tissue. She wrinkled her nose at Max. 'Both of you.'

'And we'll miss you and your – shall we say – eccentric wardrobe,' Max smiled. 'As will your mother. Both your mothers, in fact. Your mum's still in Exham, isn't she, Steve? Does your aunt know?'

Steve nodded. 'Aunt Angela says she's delighted. She's so busy with the café and her boyfriend Owen, I don't think she'll have time to miss me, although she says she's sorry to lose Mandy from the café. I have a sneaky suspicion she thinks I'm not good enough for Mandy. She said, "Mandy will easily find work in catering or marketing. She can keep you while you're a struggling musician."' He shot Mandy a look. 'Which is my plan, actually.'

Mandy reached over and punched him lightly on the arm. 'I might even start my own business – like you did, Mrs F, when you came to Exham. I'll be an entre— oh, I never can say that word.'

Max said, 'An entrepreneur? You'll go far.'

Mandy felt a weight slide off her shoulders. She looked up to Max and Libby more than she could explain. She'd hardly slept last night, afraid they'd tell her she was making a big mistake by leaving the safety of Exham-on-Sea and trying to make it in the big world. But if the two of them, who'd made such huge changes in their own lives, 'at their age' as Steve said, could do it, maybe it wasn't so scary after all.

Steve said, 'Mandy was worried you'd be mad at her. You know, after you've done so much. Letting her live here and all.'

Libby squeezed Mandy's arm. 'Not at all. It's time for you two to spread your wings, even though it means you'll be going to the bright lights and leaving us all behind in our quiet seaside backwater.'

'Not,' Steve pointed out, 'that Exham is exactly quiet. How many crimes have Ramshore and Forest, Private Investigators, solved in the past few years?'

'Good point,' Max said. 'Fortunately, the only thing we have on our books at the moment is our possibly murdered monk. Who died, as we thought, more than four hundred years ago.' He rose from the table and clapped his hands. 'And now, before we all get too sentimental, we promised the dogs a run on the beach so we'll leave you two alone. When will you be leaving for the bright lights, Mandy?'

'Well, when Libby's decided what to do with the cottage. I won't leave it empty.'

'Don't worry about that,' Max said. 'Exham-on-Sea's full of holiday makers, and whether Libby lets it to another tenant or decides to sell, it will be snapped up in less than a week. You mark my words.'

* * *

Max and Libby wandered, arm in arm, near the lighthouse. With the summer season already well under way, the dogs had to keep off the central section of the beach where a Punch and Judy Show jostled for space with myriad sandcastles.

'Mandy's leaving feels like the end of an era,' Libby said, watching Shipley racing in circles and sniffing the sand, ever hopeful of finding new and exciting smells.

'Bear's looking better,' Max pointed out. Despite taking daily tablets, Bear suffered from rheumatism and he'd learned to take life slowly. This afternoon, though, he was trotting along, ears pricked, tail in the air, like a youngster. 'The sunshine helps his old bones.'

Libby laughed. 'Thank you for trying to cheer me up. I know things change, and of course Mandy had to leave Exham at some time, but I can't help getting a bit nostalgic for the old days.'

Max stopped walking, his face stern. 'The old days before we were married, you mean?'

'Of course not. I meant, when she first moved in with me. I noticed you didn't mention that Reg was likely to join us at the abbey, on his quest for British ghosts.'

'It didn't seem quite right to drop that particular bombshell at lunch. I didn't want to spoil the, er, touching and emotional atmosphere.' Max chuckled.

'Well, I suppose you get marks for tact but none at all for romance. I hope Reg's arrival doesn't cause trouble between those two. I never knew exactly how close Mandy was to him, or how much Steve knew about their affair, but I remember her face when she first met Reg. She was completely starstruck.'

Max sat down on a tree stump that had been swept up the beach with March's spring tide. 'It looks as though this trip to the abbey will be even more interesting than I expected. I bet you won't want to miss it now, will you?'

Libby sat next to him. 'Especially as they've dated the bones. Over four hundred years doesn't give an exact date, but it would just about fit with Archie's hopes that Bernard died around the time of the dissolution of the monasteries, when the king sold them off for cash to fight the French.'

'While at the same time seizing power over the Church from the Pope so he could divorce his wife and marry Anne Boleyn. Henry VIII was quite an operator, if you ask me.' Max picked up a stick, drew a heart in the sand and scrawled their initials inside it. 'There. Don't tell me I'm not romantic.'

12

The day of the ghost hunt dawned, the skies clear, the sun beating down as though imagining it was shining over the South of France. 'But it will get cold at the abbey overnight,' Libby pointed out, trying to be practical. 'We'll need our warmest jumpers.'

She spent the morning in the café, alternating between excitement and dread.

'So,' Gladys Evans, from the flower shop, leaned against the counter. 'Tonight's the big expedition.'

Libby had known there was no way to keep it a secret. Not in Exham.

Gladys shivered. 'Rather you than me. Messing around with dead people. Not my cup of tea at all.' She shook her head, sorrowfully. 'I'll have a plate of pastries and a pot of tea, today, please. Treating myself.' She blushed, looking positively bashful.

Libby clutched her heart in mock horror. 'A whole plate? Just for you?'

Gladys whispered, 'Don't you go telling anyone, but I met a

nice man from home in the shop, yesterday.' Her Welsh accent became suddenly more pronounced. 'He'd come to get some flowers for his mother. Peonies, I sold him; my most expensive. He'll be coming in for a cup of tea in a moment.'

Libby said, 'I'll get Annabel to bring it over.' Why Gladys thought meeting her new man in the busy café was a good way to keep her affairs private, Libby had no idea, but Gladys was a mystery. Maybe this new acquaintance of hers would make her happy. She'd been a shadow of her former cheery, gossipy self since her sister died.

There was no more time to wonder about Gladys, for a queue had formed and Libby, Mandy and Annabel were run off their feet, serving. Libby's latest chocolates, displayed in the window in shiny cellophane bags, tempted passers-by into the shop to taste free samples and more often than not buy a selection. Mandy's latest suggestion, small replicas of the Low Lighthouse made from milk chocolate, were flying off the shelves. Libby's peanut butter and strawberry flavour had a more mixed reaction.

'It's like Marmite – you either love it or hate it,' Annabel said.

'Mm.' Libby thought about that. 'Marmite chocolates?'

'No,' said Mandy. 'Please. Just – no.'

Libby was going to miss Mandy's marketing flair. She stopped serving for a moment to think. She would need someone to take Mandy's place. Her heart sank at the thought of training up a new apprentice. But at least Angela would help.

Life was easier now Steve's capable aunt was managing the café, and Angela's business advice would be a real help to Mandy if she started her own business. Angela would make a terrific mentor.

'Excuse me.' Peter, the annoying young lad from the estate agency, raised his voice, breaking into Libby's reverie. 'I asked you twice, Mrs Forest. A seeded bloomer and a brie and cranberry roll, if it's not too much trouble.'

Libby slipped his order across the counter. She wished Peter were moving away, not Mandy.

Just then, her phone rang; Rory, the student from Bristol University was calling. Libby moved back into the kitchen to talk in peace.

He sounded excited. 'Mrs Forest? Charlie asked me to call you.'

He ran through the results Max had already passed on to Libby. She let him talk, wondering why he'd really called if he had nothing new to add.

Finally, Rory got to the point. 'Charlie heard your History Society are doing some ghost-hunting tonight and we wondered if we could come along.'

Libby groaned quietly. There were already far too many people planning to spend the night at the abbey. The enterprise was growing out of control. Silently, she cursed Rosalind for suggesting it. At least the woman was responsible for all the arrangements with the managers of the site. Maybe the numbers would deter any ghosts from making their appearance. Libby had been involved in too many murder investigations to enjoy chasing things that go bump in the night.

'By the way, that's not all.' Rory was still talking in her ear. 'You noticed the hole in the skull? I showed it to you.'

'Yes.' Libby held her breath.

'We think it was probably made by a blunt instrument, and it hadn't healed, which means it was inflicted at the time of his death, so—'

Libby interrupted. 'So, you think our monk came to a sticky and premature end?'

'Yeah. That's what it looks like. We think the blow on his head is a likely cause of death, and it's too small and sharp-edged to have been caused by a simple fall. So he's probably a murder victim.'

13

That evening, Libby and Max negotiated the twisting Minehead Road towards Cleeve Abbey. The sun still shone warmly and Somerset looked at its best, the bright green hedges veiled in white cow parsley, the grass alive with poppies and love-in-a-mist. All the same, Libby shifted in the passenger seat. 'I'd rather be at home, watching the sunset from our garden. Especially as Rosalind, our ghost-hunter expert, won't let us bring the dogs.'

'Reg agrees with her. He's done this sort of thing before in the States and he says the dogs will spoil the ambience.' Max slowed to join the back of a queue of cars behind an enormous tractor.

'Well, that would be fine with me,' Libby grumbled. 'I've got a bad feeling about this. Why mess with the supernatural when there's enough to worry about in real life?'

Max shot her a look. 'Do you want me to turn around? We don't have to be there.'

'And miss all the action, if there is any?' Libby grunted. 'Well done, you've called my bluff. I'm too nosy to stay away. But I reserve the right to run away screaming if anything in the least scary happens.' She thought about it. 'But I can't wait to see Reg again.'

Max said, 'Now, it's my turn to worry. I think you like him far too much. I'm beginning to get jealous.'

As the tractor pulled into a lay-by to let the traffic pass, Libby smiled, smugly. 'Excellent. That's partly why I like to have Reg around. He keeps you on your toes. And the nosy parker in me wants to know what happens when Mandy sees him again. He'd better not cause trouble between her and Steve.' She let out a sudden cry. 'Watch that deer—'

Max screeched to a halt in time for a group of red deer to trot across the road, led by a magnificently antlered stag. The stag paused in the safety of the nearby trees, turned and watched them drive away.

'I swear he's laughing at us,' Libby said.

At last, they drew up at the car park near the abbey. Three or four cars had already parked and Libby spotted Charlie sharing an animated discussion with Rory that involved a good deal of pointing and head-scratching.

Libby strolled over. 'Hi, anything wrong?'

Charlie rolled her eyes as Rory left them alone. 'That Rosalind character is driving me crazy. She can't make her mind up where to set up her equipment and she thinks there are too many people here. She says it will drive away the monks. Oh no...' She turned away. 'Here she comes again. I'm hiding in my car for a while.'

She disappeared, leaving Libby exposed to the full force of Rosalind's highly vocal annoyance. She looked around for Max, but he was talking to Archie and managed not to see his wife's pleading look.

Rosalind looked Libby up and down. 'I hope you haven't brought any more onlookers. This isn't a game, you know.'

Libby bit back a sharp reply. Rosalind was using the society meeting for her own purposes, hoping to polish her reputation as a paranormal investigator, but there was no point in saying so. Instead, she forced a friendly smile, 'You invited the members of our History Society to come along. And we're all thrilled to have you directing operations.'

She blushed. Mandy would shriek with laughter at the sarcasm, but it floated over Rosalind's head like feathers in the breeze.

The ghost-hunter-in-chief harrumphed. 'Well, at least they're interested. There are so many who choose to sneer. They don't have respect for the spiritual world.' She tucked a strand of her bright hair into its clasp at the back of her head. 'Now, there's no time to waste. I've set up my equipment, so let's get started.'

'Is there much equipment?'

'Of course. I might get a TV programme out of it.'

Libby blinked. 'I'm not sure we were expecting that. You just said you were doing some experiments. Research, we thought. We don't want to be filmed—'

'Nonsense,' Rosalind snorted. 'Everyone wants to be on TV. Anyone who objects can sign one of my forms, but I can tell you, no one ever does. In any case, I will be filming the supernatural phenomena, not you or your friends.' She turned her back on Libby and beckoned with both hands. 'Gather round, everyone.'

The group assembled in ones and twos. Charlie and Rory stood a little apart, ignoring Rosalind, as they examined a map of the abbey on Charlie's laptop.

Jemima, in her element, beamed alternately at Archie on one side, Quentin on her other. Two spots of red stood out on her cheeks.

Angela was with Mandy and Steve.

'Where's Owen?' Libby asked.

Owen, Angela's new partner, owned the Crusts and Crumbs Café. 'He's finishing up at the café,' she said. 'He's not keen on this affair. Says it's playing with fire.'

'I agree with him,' Libby said, her doubts returning. 'But there are so many of us here that I'm sure nothing will happen. Safety in numbers, you know.' Her stomach was in knots.

Beyond Charlie and Rory, Tom Reeves folded his arms, watching with narrowed eyes. His wife, Winifred, stood a little behind him, fiddling with a couple of bulging plastic shopping bags. One bag split, and a heap of variously coloured plastic containers fell on the grass. Rory stepped back to help her, accidentally kicking one of the boxes.

'My pie,' she cried, flustered, fretting as though something terrible had happened. 'It's Tom's favourite and I made it specially. It'll be shaken to bits.'

Rory handed over a container. 'What a shame.' He looked closer. 'These are just sandwiches, I think.'

'No, no, not that one,' she fussed. 'The red one over there.'

Rory patiently retrieved the pie in its container, which had landed a few metres away, and handed it over.

'No harm done,' Winifred said, relief lightening her voice, as though recovering from a crisis. 'It seems to be all right. At least it's not muddy, not with this lovely weather. Although today's been too hot for me.'

Tom sighed, ostentatiously. 'Stupid woman,' he grunted.

Libby whispered to Max, 'I wish Tom Reeves would lighten up. Look at poor Winifred. She's like a little mouse, making such a fuss about dropping his supper. I think she's scared of him.'

Rosalind raised her voice before Max could reply. 'I want all of you in groups of two or three and I'll position you in the best spots. You'll be responsible for watching and listening – oh, for heaven's sake, what now?'

Two more cars had driven up. DC Gemma Humberstone jumped out of one and joined the group. Ian Smith followed more slowly.

Mandy stiffened. 'Who invited him?' she muttered to Gemma.

'He's on the monk's bones case. He thinks he'll get paid overtime for tonight.'

Max chuckled. 'Not if I know DCI Morrison.'

But Libby's eyes were on the other car. The door flew open and Reg loped across the grass, a broad smile slashing his face in half.

'Long time no see.' He gathered Libby in a warm hug and kissed her on either cheek. 'So Max finally persuaded you to marry him,' he drawled. 'Lucky man.'

'Actually,' Max pointed out, 'she proposed to me.'

But Libby wasn't listening. She was watching Mandy.

Mandy's face, already pale, had turned ashen. Her mouth hung open.

Reg caught sight of her and stiffened. 'Well, if it isn't my favourite Goth.' He recovered and threw an arm around Mandy's shoulders. 'Great to see you again. And you must be Steve.'

Steve gulped. He'd been living in London when Reg was in Exham. Libby wondered again how much Mandy had told him about her fling with Reg. He knew something, judging by his frown.

Reg towered over him, put out a hand and engulfed Steve's fingers in his own.

Rosalind called the group back to attention, rescuing Steve from the awkward moment. 'If everyone's here – at last.' She glared at the latest arrivals.

Libby chuckled. Rosalind didn't know Gemma and Ian were with the police. She was disappointed when they produced their warrant cards.

While Rosalind huffed and puffed, Mandy muttered under her breath, 'I'm not being "positioned" anywhere near Ian Smith.'

Reg looked puzzled. 'He's a bit fat and greasy, but what's the guy done to you?'

'He pinched her bottom once and she threw a chocolate cream at him,' Max said.

'Attagirl.' Admiration warmed Reg's voice. 'Still the same fireball.'

Steve narrowed his eyes. 'Smith won't be doing anything like that while I'm around,' he said, 'even if he is the police.'

'My hero,' Mandy said, shooting a sideways glance at Reg.

'If I may have everyone's attention.' Rosalind glared round the group, her hands on her hips. Her hair was slipping out from its bindings, adhering stickily to her forehead.

Max murmured, 'She's going to explode.'

Rosalind held up the waiver forms.

Gemma said, 'We can't be in any of your camera shots, I'm afraid, and we're here on business about the bones, so we'll need to see any footage you take, and any participants here today will need to give their permission before you can use it.'

Charlie joined in, 'I'm here on behalf of the university, and you'll have to clear any of your work with them. There will be legal restrictions on what you can put on air.'

Rosalind, lips tightly pursed, waved a hand vaguely, as though this were all nonsense. 'Yes, yes, very well. Whatever you say. This is just exploratory, anyway. Nothing's going to happen with so many folk chattering.'

Libby smiled. It seemed Rosalind had bitten off more than she could chew with Exham folk.

14

At last, the Exham ghost hunters had grouped themselves in locations that Rosalind, her bossy attitude in retreat, thought were likely to yield results. 'The spirits will want quiet spaces, where they feel safe.'

'Codswallop,' Max said.

Reg snorted. 'Is that a real word?' He was with Libby and Max in a tiny room to the south of the old abbey building, surrounded by Max's rugs and Libby's picnic hamper. Crows flew past the entrance, cawing harshly as they returned to their nests high in the nearby trees.

'Don't you say that in America?' Libby asked.

'Ah, the old story, two countries separated by a common language,' Reg sighed, 'as somebody once said.'

Jemima, with the two men Libby now thought of as her admirers, had made herself comfortable upstairs in the refectory. Angela took Mandy and Steve to the dormitory, while Rosalind ushered Tom and Winifred Reeves into another small room on the ground floor. 'The Chapter house,' she announced loudly. 'Where the monks settled their arguments.'

Gemma insisted she and Ian needed the freedom to roam at will.

Rosalind, clearly at the end of her tether, held her head in her hands. 'Just do it quietly, please,' she groaned.

Charlie and Rory passed Libby and Max, carrying sleeping bags and thermos flasks.

'You look as though you've done this before,' Libby said.

Charlie nodded. 'Once or twice. Not here, but in other ancient buildings.'

'And?'

Charlie shrugged. 'Nothing. Not a hint of anything paranormal.'

'But you never know,' Rory said.

A peaceful murmur of voices hummed through the grounds of the abbey as the hungry ghost-hunters ate sandwiches and poured tea. Several had brought wine and beer. 'Half of them will be asleep by midnight,' Max declared.

'I don't blame them,' Libby said. 'Pour me a glass of white wine, please. It may be the first of several.'

Reg said, 'I bought the guidebook. I gather Henry VIII kicked the monks out over some religious dispute with Europe.'

'It wasn't really about religion at all, but about Henry wanting to divorce his wife and move on to another,' Libby explained. 'Every schoolchild in England learns about Henry's six wives.'

Reg nodded. 'I know the story. A couple of those wives came to sticky ends.'

Max put in, 'Talking of marriages, Reg, are you on your second or third?'

Reg shrugged. 'In between three and four. My recent wedding was a big mistake – turned out Crystal wasn't satisfied with just one man. She had a few more stacked up in reserve.'

Max roared with unsympathetic laughter. 'Sounds like Anne Boleyn herself.'

Libby watched Reg carefully. Was his arrival in England just as his marriage crumbled a coincidence? Surely, it wasn't Mandy that had brought him here? She was twenty years his junior and Libby had never been happy when they'd been – well, what had they been doing, a few years ago? Courting? Having an affair? Libby had been close to Mandy, and still was, but they'd never talked much about that time.

She wrenched her thoughts back to the present. Reg was whistling over the vast sums of money Henry had raised by dissolving the monasteries. 'Ruthless, that guy.'

'Absolutely,' Max agreed. 'Cleeve Abbey was sold off early and all the monks sent away.'

'And has anyone seen ghosts here?'

'Well, there are stories. A Christmas visitor once thought he heard footsteps and voices. He wrote about it on Facebook.'

An involuntary shiver ran up Libby's spine. 'I'm hoping he was making it all up. I really don't want to meet anything spooky.'

A car chose that moment to screech to a halt outside. Libby started, her wine splashing on the flagstones.

Her heart rate slowed as she heard the slam of un-ghostly car doors. She stepped outside their room and walked to the corner, looking across to the gatehouse.

That was a big mistake. A figure came through the gatehouse and waved at her.

'Oh no. Not again. The bad penny,' she groaned, as Chesterton Wendlebury strode towards her, his yellow waistcoat bright in the evening twilight.

'Now then, what's going on here? Anyone like to explain?' he boomed.

'Mr Wendlebury,' Gemma showed him her card. 'We have permission to be here. Do you?'

'Dash it all, I was just wondering what was going on, dear lady. All these cars zooming past my house at this time of night. Everyone's usually gone by now. Place closes at six, normally, you know.'

'Well, we're very pleased you're taking such an interest in the area,' Gemma smiled.

'Not the only one. Seems our sleuths are here again. All to do with those bones, I suppose. I saw the latest in the local paper. Interesting. Then, seeing the activity, I thought I'd come and see if there was room for a chap like me. Local, you know.'

'Local criminal,' Libby told Reg quietly.

'Minor criminal,' Max added. 'Harmless.'

Wendlebury looked so pleased to be there that Libby felt suddenly sorry for him. It must be hard, coming out of prison. He'd said he lived nearby, but where? He used to live near Wells. Did he own a house or had he lost everything in the fraud case?

Without making a conscious decision, she heard herself issue

an invitation to join the group. 'We've plenty of food.' They'd
better keep the whisky away from him.

'Jolly kind, don't mind if I do. A spot of company will be just
the thing for half an hour or so. Won't intrude any longer.' His
face, noticeably thinner than before his prison sentence, broke
into a smile.

He followed Libby to their corner and settled on one of the
rugs.

'Ghosts, eh?' he said. 'That'll be a turn-up for the books.'

Max engaged him in polite conversation. Reg's eyes were
sparkling, as though Wendlebury was an especially amusing
specimen of Englishness. *Which*, Libby thought, *I suppose he is.*

'Landed gentry, come down in the world,' she whispered
to Reg.

She raised her voice. She had questions, but wasn't sure how
to phrase them delicately.

'Mr Wendlebury—'

'Oh, do call me Ches, dear lady. We're old friends.'

We really aren't, she thought.

She cleared her throat. 'You live around here, now?'

'You mean, since I left my short spell at Her Majesty's
expense?' His booming laugh echoed around the stone walls of
their room. 'No need to tiptoe around, everyone knows I ended
up in prison. I made a few bad choices, I confess. But that's all
water under the bridge. I did my crime, as the lads inside would
say, and did my time. Quite the experience, you know.' He rubbed
his nose. 'They're an interesting bunch in prison. I helped one of
them write home. Poor fellow, never learned to read, no wonder
he ended up inside.'

Libby offered him a sandwich, trying to imagine Wendlebury
patiently taking dictation. She remembered he'd once pulled her
car out of a ditch. Perhaps he had redeeming features, after all.

'Don't mind if I do,' he said, selecting a baguette containing chorizo, tomato and halloumi, and swallowing half in one gulp. 'Mm, interesting sandwich. You haven't lost your touch since marrying this fellow, Mrs Forest. Now, what was I saying. Well, they let me out – plenty of time off for good behaviour, don't you know – but I had a problem with housing – can't get a mortgage, not now, and don't have much in the way of ready cash, not being gainfully employed, you see.' He wiped tomato from his chin. 'Luckily, a cousin of mine lets me rent his place, Priory Manor, and deal with some housing plans he's drawn up. He lives in London, keeps a second home on Exmoor.' His face crinkled into a smile. 'You'll never guess what he does for a living. Go on, try...'

'Solicitor? Accountant?' she hazarded.

'Not quite – worse than that... He's a politician.' That laugh boomed out again, and suddenly he was the Chesterton Wendlebury that Libby remembered – full of self-confidence and just a bit scary. 'He lets me live here, so long as I never talk about our relationship, so I can't tell you his name, I'm afraid. My lips are sealed.' He put a fat finger to his lips. 'Still, it's kind of him, and the house is comfortable. Nice part of the world, isn't it? Quiet.' He heaved his bulk off the floor. 'Now, I'm going to find a spot for myself. Might have a little snooze in a corner. Wake me if anything happens, won't you?' and he was gone, settling down in the next room.

Just then, Rosalind appeared in the open doorway, looked around and nodded. 'Good, all well here. Now, if anything happens tonight, ring this bell. Every group has one. Don't ring too loud, we don't want to frighten away any psychic manifestation, but we don't want to miss them, either. And take this camera. It's infrared and it will see things you can't.'

Max said, 'Like a night rifle sight.'

Rosalind frowned. 'Nothing so violent. The monks in this

abbey were Cistercians. Very devout and law-abiding. No talking, only occasional visitors. Definitely no fighting. Anyway, give a little tinkle on your bell if you see anything interesting. Otherwise, do keep the noise down,' she admonished as she left.

'Bossy woman.' Libby looked at her watch. 'It's only ten o'clock. This is going to be a long night.'

Reg stood and stretched. 'I'm going for a wander. I can use the light on my phone if I need to.'

'Don't you think we should stay together?' Libby asked. 'Just in case – you know...' she hesitated.

'In case a mad monk creeps up behind me?' Reg chuckled. 'I can look after myself, you know.'

Libby and Max fell silent as he left, listening and watching, peering into the gloom. The white arches of the roof seemed to rise out of the darkness, shimmering a little. Libby thought of the monks, sleeping in rows in their dormitory at night, trooping down a narrow, twisting staircase in silence to pray, then coming back to sleep for a few more hours before the next service in the chapel. What a life.

Wrapped in blankets, leaning against Max, Libby was lulled into a kind of in-between land, neither awake nor asleep. She tried to keep her eyes open, wondering if she might catch sight of one of the monks. White robes, that was what they wore, she remembered. Really, there would be nothing worrying about seeing one, just one, gliding past in silence.

The abbey exuded peace, its walls mellowed by centuries of prayer. What was it Cleeva had said in her pamphlet? Only good ghosts, here.

Relaxed and happy, Libby dozed.

Winifred Reeves watched her husband anxiously. Tom was like a smouldering fire, ready to burst into flames at any moment. Still, that was nothing new. He seemed to be angry all the time, these days.

She unpacked the provisions she'd brought; a bottle of his favourite brand of whisky; plenty of sandwiches filled with ham, cheese and salad; packets of crisps and cheesy snacks; bars of Cadbury's chocolate; three different flavours of yoghurt and his favourite apple pie, still largely intact. That selection should please him, surely? If anything could.

If only she could do something to make him happy. He'd been such fun when they first married. He'd been busy working hard on their tiny farm, but she'd worked alongside him when she wasn't teaching in the little local primary school. They hadn't been rich, but they'd been happy, even though Tom always had some story that his family had once been cheated out of their land. Mind you, half the families in the area thought the richest families had stolen their land. Something to do with the enclosure of common farm land by the local bigwigs, if she remembered rightly.

And then, Freddy was born. Tom's face had lit up like the sun, that day. There were years of father-son trips to the football, and teenage parties in the shed, with hay bales, bunting and loud music. Tom and Freddy hadn't always seen eye-to-eye, of course, and they'd had their share of shouting matches, but when Freddy had decided to move to London, they'd let him go. After all, he'd moved into a flat with his cousin and a bunch of friends and had a job in a bar. It seemed safe, exciting, even. Winifred had envied him a little.

Then, disaster struck.

Winifred tried so hard not to think about that. She'd tucked Freddy's death away in the box she kept in her head, and she managed, most days, to keep the box shut tight. But when Tom was unbearable, as he had been lately, it became harder than ever to stop herself opening the box and thinking about Freddy, wondering what was left in life without her only son. She saw the years stretching ahead, full of Tom's bitter anger and her loneliness and she wasn't sure she wanted to keep going.

She fumbled in her bag and offered Tom a sandwich. She'd hoped he'd enjoy the ghost hunt – that it might bring him out of himself a bit. She'd persuaded him to come along, even though he disliked her sister. 'Rosalind thinks she's better than us,' he said. 'What with her big house and her posh husband and son at university and all.'

Houses were the focus of Tom's current anger; in particular, the Wendlebury family's plans for a small housing estate on Priory Manor land. Tom had a particular dislike of the Wendleburys. Crooks, he'd always called them. When Chesterton Wendlebury had gone to prison, Tom had been delighted. She'd hoped he'd forget about it, in tonight's excitement, but he'd caught sight of Chesterton Wendlebury arriving at the abbey and that had been the last straw.

'Don't worry about the planning committee, for now,' she said. 'It doesn't really matter.' She was convinced there was no way to change the local council's mind.

'Of course it matters, woman. That land has the best trout river in the county, and the oak wood dates back to William the Conqueror.'

'1066,' Winifred murmured, before she could stop herself.

Tom glared. 'I'm not one of your primary school kids.'

'Sorry.'

'And don't keep saying sorry all the time. Grow a backbone, can't you?'

'I'm s—' she cut herself off and unwrapped a second sandwich.

Winifred's head throbbed. She hoped she wasn't starting a migraine. She took a long drink of water.

She'd looked forward to this evening, reading as much as she could find about the abbey, planning which areas she'd visit. It would be like old times, when they'd brought Freddy here as a boy. He'd been quite a handful, climbing on top of the remains of the walls, running up and down the monks' stairs and jumping over the rope barrier to walk on the ancient tiled floor of the ruined chapel.

The old memory brought a smile to her face. 'Do you remember when Freddy threatened to jump out of one of the upstairs windows?' she asked, trying to divert Tom.

It was too late. Tom was up on his hobby horse and there was no stopping him.

Winifred took a bite from the salad wrap she'd brought for herself. Maybe if she stuck to her latest diet and lost a bit of

weight, Tom would have more time for her. He'd loved her trim
figure once, back in the day.

'What you don't understand, Winifred,' he said, 'is that the
Wendleburys have always had life easy, with all those acres of
farmland.'

Winifred had stopped listening. She'd heard Tom rant about
the Wendleburys owning land so often before.

He went on, regardless, 'They don't appreciate them. When
Laurence Wendlebury got himself elected – and I bet he had to
stump up a few back-handers for that – I thought he'd forget
about those plans for chopping down the trees and building on
his land. Maybe he would have, if his cousin hadn't come out of
prison and Laurence came over all soft, letting Chesterton
manage the estate. Before we know it, Winifred,' he tapped a
finger on his knee, 'there'll be houses like little boxes all over
West Somerset and nowhere left to walk at all. Nowhere.' He
scrubbed at his face with a grubby hand. 'It's not as though the
houses will be any good for local people. They'll all be second
homes for Londoners with more money than sense.'

Winifred touched his arm. 'It won't bring Freddy back, you
know, fighting the plans. You won't win against the Wendleburys.
Freddy would know that. When he left home, he told you not to
take life so seriously.'

'He didn't take it serious enough, did he? Getting run over by
a taxi, like a fool. He should have stayed here, in Somerset, safe
with us.' Tom's face softened a little. 'He loved the woods and the
streams, did Freddy. Making dens with his mates and dipping for
minnows. Played for hours, until it was dark and we had to drag
him home.' Tom sniffed and his voiced hardened. 'He should
have stayed here, rented a little house, got married and settled
down. No good comes of moving to London.'

Winifred sighed. If only Tom would lose that chip on his shoulder.

He stabbed his finger at her face. 'I'll save the woods from Wendlebury, in memory of Freddy, no matter what happens.' He took a savage bite from his baguette. 'You forgot the mustard again, woman,' he grumbled.

She froze. What was that?

There it was, again.

Winifred leapt to her feet. 'Come on, Tom. That's one of the bells. Hurry.'

17

BELLS

From all sides, the ghost hunters came running, in ones and twos, breathless, waving torches and phone lights, crowding together in the cloister.

'Did you hear that?' Reg asked.

'Who rang their bell?' Rosalind demanded.

No one spoke.

Rosalind looked around the blank faces. She groaned and raised clenched fists to her head. 'Every time,' she moaned. 'Every single time, someone has to ring their bell when it gets dark. It's not funny, you know. Or clever.' She looked from one face to another, counting. 'There are people missing.'

Max said, 'Where's Ian Smith? We might have known he'd be up to something.'

'I thought he was with you,' Libby said to Gemma.

Gemma shook her head. 'He insisted on taking a torch and going off on his own.'

'But where is he?' Anxious, Libby flashed her torch in all directions. Had something happened to him?

Suddenly, Reg laughed and pointed, 'There he is.'

PC Ian Smith emerged from his hiding place, at the foot of a disused staircase. He was bent double with laughter. 'Got you all, good and proper. I wish you could see your faces.'

No one in the cloister found it at all funny.

Rosalind said, 'If you can't behave, young man, I'll have to ask you to leave.'

'Sorry, ma'am,' Ian was unrepentant. 'I'm the police and I'm here to ensure everyone's safety. Call that a drill. Like a fire alarm.' He snorted with laughter. 'Glad to see you're all present and correct,' he said and sauntered away, grinning.

Gemma gave a long-suffering sigh. 'It's OK, everyone. Nothing to worry about. We're all here, safe and sound.'

Libby and Max trailed back to their corner. On the way, Libby started to see the funny side. 'He's quite right. We looked like a band of scared cats, all glowing eyes and heavy breathing.'

'Stupid man,' Max said. 'It's hard to believe he's still with the police. Talk about a bad apple.'

'To be honest,' Libby said, 'I feel a bit safer knowing Ian and Gemma are here, even if they're unofficial. They'll make sure there's no funny business tonight.'

* * *

'I'm going to stay outside and look up at the stars.' As they dispersed, Charlie wandered away from the others. The stars were clear in the sky and she was keen to enjoy them on this cloudless night. She opened up her laptop to a stargazer page to be sure what she was looking for. What a shame no meteor showers were due tonight. The conditions were perfect.

She had no idea how long she sat cross-legged on the grass, her back resting against the bricks of the abbey. The temperature had dropped, now the sun had gone down, and a chilly breeze had sprung up. She pulled her old green blanket around her shoulders. It was like being a child again, shivering through the night, while her father pointed out Orion's Belt and The Plough, far up in the sky.

Stargazing gave her time to think tonight, away from Rory. Not that she had anything against her student. He'd come to the university later than most of the others, after a couple of years in an IT business start-up in London, and he was working hard for approval. She felt a little mean leaving him alone, but his puppyish enthusiasm could be draining. He was so proud of himself for uncovering the evidence of the monk's profession.

She sighed. At least the bone discovery would help her career. She'd been looking for a suitable topic for a paper, and the mysterious monk fit the bill very well. A sighting of a ghostly monk would be the icing on the cake, but, of course, it was all nonsense. Nothing Charlie had seen had convinced her of the existence of ghosts.

Still, said the little, hopeful voice in her head. *You never know.*

In the dormitory, Mandy was restless. 'I'm going for a walk. Otherwise, I'll fall asleep. It's already past midnight and I can't eat another thing.'

'I'm still hungry,' Steve complained. 'And there are two slices of fruit cake left. Wait a minute, and I'll come with you.'

'You can catch me up,' Mandy suggested. 'I bet I get a photo of a monk while you're still stuffing your face.'

'I bet you a thousand quid you don't see anything.'

'You haven't got that much dosh.'

'I won't need it.'

Angela sighed, heavily. 'Do stop bickering, you two. Mandy, if you must go off on your own, be sensible and wrap up warm. Don't run on the stairs – they're none of them especially safe.'

Mandy tied her scarlet cloak securely around her neck.

Steve, wolfing down his final mouthful, said, 'I've finished eating. I'll come with you.'

But she'd already gone.

* * *

Mandy slipped quickly down the stairs and set off across the grass, towards the gatehouse. She'd been mean, dashing away before Steve could finish eating his cake, but she needed time on her own, to think.

Reg's appearance had shaken her to the core. If only she'd known he was coming, she could have prepared herself. As it was, she'd had trouble hiding her shaky hands from Steve when she caught sight of Reg.

She'd never told Steve much about her time with Reg. Until today, it had all seemed like a dream. The kind of daydream you have when you're a teenager and you imagine a tall, exotic stranger falling in love with you.

She'd even moved in with Reg in Bristol for a while. Luckily, few people knew that. She'd pretended to Exham folk she was staying with her mother. She'd quarrelled with Libby, because she'd failed to turn up for work one day, but she'd apologised and they'd never mentioned it again. She was sure Libby and Max knew about the infatuation with Reg, but they'd never poked their noses too far into Mandy's business. In any case, it was just an infatuation, wasn't it?

Mandy looked out of the archway, towards the river. It was very quiet here in the gatehouse. The tension in her throat relaxed. She was older now than when she'd known Reg. Older and wiser. She could look back at herself as though seeing another person, and wish she'd had more sense in those days.

Of course Reg hadn't come to England now to find her. When he left, he'd gone home to marry a woman nearer his own age. Crystal, that was her name. Sophisticated, elegant and expensive, like the champagne. Mandy's exact opposite.

Mandy had struggled to hide her broken heart when they'd quarrelled and broken up. She'd spent hours alone in her room, wondering whether she and Reg had made a mistake.

But she'd been right to stick to her guns. Steve accepted her for herself, while she'd often felt Reg wanted to change her, trying to persuade her to stop dressing like a Goth, or playing Siouxsie and the Banshees too loudly. She stuck out her chin. A Goth was who she was; unconventional, a free spirit, not caring what other people thought, even though unconventional people rarely undertook catering apprenticeships and spent their life baking scones in a small seaside town. Now, though, she was about to leave all that behind, and step into the big wide world in London.

She took a deep breath, drinking in the warm night air. There was so much to think about and Steve would find her at any moment. She loved Steve. She wanted to make her life with him. Steve never objected to the way she dressed. She felt a warm smile spread across her face, and knew Reg had been just an adolescent fantasy. Steve was her best friend, and she loved him. Soon they'd move to London together. She had everything she wanted.

Just then, Mandy heard a noise.

She turned round, but there was no one in the gatehouse. The noise must have been an owl. She swung back, peering into the darkness outside, fumbling with her torch. Her heart pounded. She could feel it thudding in her chest.

A crack, like thunder, exploded in her head. She stumbled, clutching at the wall, her ears ringing.

Another voice cried out. She turned to look, but she'd dropped her torch and could see nothing in the dark but a blur.

She stumbled again, trying to get away, out of the gatehouse, but her legs refused to move. For a long moment, she stood, swaying, until her legs gave way altogether and blackness closed in.

The clock struck two. Libby jerked awake. She'd fallen asleep, despite her best intentions, sitting uncomfortably with her back against the wall and a chill creeping up from her feet.

'It's all right,' Max said. 'It's just the clock.'

'I wish it wouldn't do that. It made me jump.' She struggled into a more comfortable position, wiggling her toes inside her boots. 'Whose bright idea was this anyway? And where's Reg?'

'Nipped out for a moment.'

'Again? He's got ants in his pants. I hope he's not making trouble between Mandy and Steve.'

'I doubt it. I'm sure he's moved on since his affair with Mandy.'

Someone loomed into view, waving a torch.

Libby blinked, trying to see who it was. 'Rosalind?'

Rosalind hissed, 'There's something interesting happening in the refectory.'

'What? And where's the refectory?' Libby felt disorientated.

'North side of the cloister. Come quickly, but don't make a

noise. And don't wave your torch about. We might have a sighting.'

Libby caught her breath, suddenly excited. What could possibly happen while they were all together?

As silently as possible, which meant a certain amount of hushed giggling and an occasional muffled curse, Libby and Max left the space that had begun to feel like home and made their way down a passage and up the stairs to the refectory. Libby tried hard to remember who'd chosen that particular place to wait. 'If this is Ian Smith again,' she murmured in Max's ear, 'I'll have something to say.'

'It won't be. It was moderately funny once, but not twice.'

'I don't know. Ian has no common sense.'

Rosalind turned. 'Stop talking,' she said softly. 'You'll frighten them away.'

Libby slapped her hand over her own mouth to block a snort of hysterical laughter. 'Scared ghosts? This gets dafter all the time.'

As they slipped into the refectory, Angela joined them. 'Mandy and Steve have gone off. I've no idea what they're up to and I don't really want to find out.'

'I think we can guess,' Max said.

In moments, a group had gathered, huddling together at the top of the stairs, all torches turned off.

'Look. Over there.' That was Jemima's voice. She was pointing to the west side of the refectory.

Libby narrowed her eyes, trying to see through the gloom. Was that a shape, moving along the wall? She blinked hard. There was definitely something there. Or was it her imagination?

To her right, Rosalind was operating an infrared camera.

The shape swirled. Was it real? Was that a monk's hood over

its face? For a second, Libby was almost sure she'd seen something, but then it was gone.

Excited, the group buzzed and muttered.

'It's cold,' someone said.

Libby half-turned to check who it was, but before she could see, an unearthly cry sounded from outside.

'Ian!' someone called, threateningly, 'Is that you?'

The hush in the refectory was broken as the group turned from one to the other, asking, 'Did you hear it?' 'What was that?'

The cry came again.

'It's coming from the gatehouse,' Rosalind gasped, turning and hurrying down the steps, the rest following as fast as they could in the dark.

They ran across the grass, and the cries were louder. 'Someone help us.'

Angela shouted, 'Steve?' and ran ahead, through the archway into the gatehouse. 'What's going on?'

Steve was kneeling by Mandy's body.

In moments, everyone was crammed inside the gatehouse, jostling to see what had happened.

Mandy's figure lay, motionless, on the flagstones, almost completely hidden by her scarlet cloak.

Gemma waved everyone aside. 'Someone call an ambulance,' she commanded.

Steve looked up, his face white in the darkness. 'She's not breathing.' His voice croaked.

Ian, suddenly serious, said, 'I'll take over – you stand back.' He leaned over Mandy's still, silent body, pressing on her chest, counting, and then breathing into her mouth.

Libby, her stomach heaving, grasped Max's hand. 'She's not going to die, is she?' she muttered. 'Not Mandy.' She swallowed hard.

'What happened? Does anyone know?' Max asked.

Angela was next to Libby, her whole body shaking. 'Steve followed her here, to see if she was OK. She'd gone off on her own, you see.'

'Steve,' Gemma said, 'do you know what happened?'

He said nothing, too busy watching Ian Smith to respond.

'Right,' Gemma went on, 'I've called it in. We'll have back-up soon and an ambulance. Don't leave the abbey. Everyone will have to make a statement.'

Libby tried to gather her wits. Was everyone here? She counted. They were all accounted for, now, but had one of them sneaked up on Mandy and joined them later? She peered from one face to another in the light of the torches. Who could it be? And why attack Mandy?

'What's that?' Gemma was training her torch on a spot just beside Mandy's leg. She laid the torch on the flagstones, positioned so that its light still fell on the same spot. She bent down, pulling a plastic bag from her pocket. With her other hand, she used a pen to dislodge a piece of paper that glimmered in the torchlight and dropped it into the bag.

'What is it?' Max knelt beside her and Libby followed.

Gemma glanced at him, as though on the verge of telling him it was none of his business. She sighed. 'I suppose I can let you look. You're almost one of us.'

She held out the bag, flattening it and the paper inside.

The paper held a single printed sentence.

Gatehouse one o'clock good news.

A chill had fallen over the small crowd. In silence, they glanced at each other and looked away, their faces barely visible in the light of torches and mobile phones. Their unspoken thoughts were written in their wide eyes, slack jaws and wrinkled foreheads.

Libby grasped Max's hand. Someone had lured Mandy to the chapel deliberately, intent on attacking – killing – her. And that someone was here, now, watching.

When Libby awoke, next morning, she'd forgotten what had happened. She yawned. Why was she so tired? And why was she back home, wasn't she ghost-hunting...?

And then it hit her, with the force of a punch to the stomach.

Mandy. Mandy who was like a daughter to her, lying on the cold floor, unconscious. She'd started breathing as the ambulance arrived, but Libby had no idea how badly she was hurt. Her stomach churned.

She sat up straight. Max was already downstairs. She could hear him clattering in the kitchen.

Her head ached. Once the police had arrived at the abbey, the ghost hunters had each given a short statement before being allowed to leave, but Libby could hardly remember what she'd said. Who had been there? She tried to remember.

Struggling into a dressing gown, she slipped downstairs. Bear sat quietly at the bottom of the stairs, waiting for her. He could always sense the mood of his favourite humans and stayed close by her side whenever she was upset.

Shipley was out in the garden, practising his rabbit-detecting skills.

'Coffee?' Max suggested, holding out a mug.

Libby took it in silence.

'Try not to panic,' Max said. 'The paramedics were very optimistic.'

'They said it was a blow to the head,' Libby heard her own voice echo dully.

'Angela will tell us what's going on. She went to the hospital with Steve.'

Steve.

Libby rubbed her forehead. It ached, from lack of sleep.

Steve had found the body.

Libby gave herself a shake. There was no point in trying to guess what had happened. She would leave it to the police. Gemma was there, and Ian Smith. He might be the most useless of DCI Morrison's team, but he'd been able to help with the interviews.

'I'll make omelettes,' Libby said. Cooking always calmed her in moments of crisis. It made life seem more normal.

Her phone rang and she snatched it up.

'Angela, what news?'

Max's phone trilled jauntily at the same time, the bright tune out of keeping with their moods.

'DCI Morrison,' he mouthed at Libby, but she was listening to her friend.

Angela sounded exhausted. 'She's still with us,' she said. Libby, suddenly sick with relief, sank onto a kitchen stool. 'They took her in to operate.'

'So, is she going to be all right?'

'They hope so.' Only hope? Was Mandy still in danger? 'She was hit on the head, maybe with a lump of stone. Part of the gatehouse, I suppose.' Angela's voice shook. 'But they're operating to fix a bleed inside her brain. They're worried about... about brain damage.' There was silence on the phone for a few seconds. Angela's voice was back under control when she spoke again. 'She's still in surgery.'

Libby swallowed hard. What could she say? She'd been involved with murders and attempted murders before, but this one was too close to home. She closed her eyes. 'It's really not an accident, then?'

'No. I hoped it might be. I thought that whoever sent Mandy the note would own up, and they'd tell us they saw her, told her this mysterious news, and left her, and she tripped over somehow, and hit her head.'

'The back of her head? I don't think so.'

'I know, it's ridiculous. But I can't believe anyone would do this deliberately.' Angela heaved a sigh. 'My head's spinning, trying to imagine what happened. You and Max will sort this out, won't you? We're counting on you.'

'I promise. Even if it kills us,' Libby said. She caught her breath. 'Sorry. That was a stupid thing to stay, but you know what I mean. How's Steve taking it?'

'He stayed with me last night – well, what was left of the night by the time we got home from the hospital. He wanted to stay but the nurses said there would be no news until this morning. I gave him one of my sleeping pills, so he's still in bed.'

There was a pause.

'Libby, I know the police will do what they can. But... but I'll be relying on you and Max.'

With that, Angela rang off. Libby stared at her phone, sharing her friend's distress.

Biting back tears, she dropped the phone in her bag and tried to distract herself with the omelettes.

As she cracked eggs, the horror of last night running through her head, Max returned. She filled him in on the details. By the time she'd finished, he looked almost as distressed as she felt.

'Morrison's asking us to call in to the station one morning,' he said. 'He wants us to help him out with Mandy's case. It's not a murder investigation, thank heaven.'

Libby took a long, shuddering breath.

'Sorry, that was tactless,' Max said.

'But you're right,' she said. 'He won't have all the resources he'd have if... if she'd been killed.' She swung round and clung to her husband. 'We were there, Max. On the spot. I can't believe it happened right under our noses. If we can't figure out who attacked Mandy, we've no right to call ourselves investigators. I just hope...'

He nodded. 'I know. Let's hope it wasn't anyone we like who attacked her.'

Libby served the omelettes. 'Mushroom. Brain food.'

'Is it?'

'Well, we need to eat, although, to be honest, I don't have much of an appetite.'

After a few mouthfuls, they both laid down their forks. 'Delicious, as always,' Max said.

'I know – but it sticks in the throat, doesn't it.' Libby pushed her plate away. 'I feel a bit better, though. Mandy's alive, and in safe hands at the hospital. We can help her most by finding the attacker.'

'Especially as, if he—'

'Or she,' Libby put in.

Max agreed. 'Let's call the attacker "they", shall we? I was going to say, as Mandy's still with us, we need to get a move on and find her attacker, because—'

'Because we don't want them to find out she's okay and have another try.'

'Exactly. Are you due at the café?'

Libby shook her head. 'Not today. I offered to go, but Angela's determined to go in herself. She says she'd rather work than sit around all day, worrying. She's planning to drop Steve at his mother's house on her way. Annabel will help her hold the fort at the café with a couple of the holiday girls. Angela wants me to spend all my time on this.'

Max's face wore a thoughtful expression. 'You know, it can't be that hard. Everyone was in small groups most of the time. So it won't be difficult to find out who was on their own and had an opportunity to attack Mandy. All we need to do is work out who was alone and when. The attacker's left us a huge clue with the note.'

'But the note was computer printed. It could have come from anyone.'

'Yes, but it tells us that Mandy knew her attacker – they had some kind of relationship – although not necessarily a close one. Maybe they had an argument we don't know about.'

Libby shot Max a horrified look.

He touched his finger to her lips. 'I know what you're thinking, but don't say anything, yet. We mustn't jump to conclusions. That's how the wrong people get blamed. We need to think through everyone there last night, how well each of them know Mandy and what the "news" the note mentioned might be. Tease out the motive.'

Libby shook her head. 'You're talking as though Mandy's dead. She's not. She'll be able to tell us what happened.' Of course, Mandy was going to be all right. Libby wasn't going to imagine anything else. She couldn't bear to even think about it.

Max opened his mouth, and closed it again. 'She will,' he

agreed, but the tremor in his voice chilled Libby's heart. 'I'm sure she will, but we won't wait. We're going to find this man.'

'Or woman,' Libby put in.

'To look on the bright side,' he said, 'I'm sure Morrison's team will pull together the forensics – fingerprints, and so on.' His smile reassured Libby not at all.

'I bet there won't be anything useful. The attacker would surely have been wearing gloves,' she said. 'Everyone knows about forensic examination these days. Only an idiot would leave their DNA on a weapon.'

'Anyway,' Max insisted, although his expression was bleak, 'I reckon we'll have this case cracked by the end of next week, and Mandy will be safely back, telling the tale to everyone in the Crusts and Crumbs and enjoying every moment.'

Libby pressed her lips together. If only she could be sure of that.

'Do you think,' Libby asked, 'that the attack on Mandy could possibly have anything to do with finding the monk's bones?' They were walking up Brent Knoll that afternoon, hoping the fresh air and light breeze would clear their heads.

'I don't know.' Max said. 'At least she's come through the surgery.'

'Angela's doing a great job,' Libby said. 'She's been fielding inquiries in the café all day, as well as constantly ringing the hospital. Everyone's so shocked. Steve's at the hospital, now, with his mother, by the way, so Angela can get some proper sleep tonight.'

Their phones had rung constantly. Reg had been first to get in touch, audibly distraught as he spoke to Max. 'I think he still has feelings for Mandy,' Max had said as the call ended. 'I wonder what really happened between those two. He's not giving anything away.'

Libby had looked hard at Max. 'You don't think...?'

'That Reg hit her? No. Never – at least – we said we'd keep open minds, didn't we. I'd find it hard to believe Reg, our friendly gentle giant, would do such a thing, but we can't discount him just because we like him.'

'And the same goes for all the others at the abbey last night.'

By lunchtime, every member of the History Society had called, wondering how anyone could have attacked Mandy. They'd each had a theory, and Libby had listened to them all. After all, Angela was relying on her to solve the mystery. But after hours spent focusing entirely on the attack on Mandy, Libby felt emotionally drained.

She'd persuaded Max to walk up the Knoll for some fresh air. The dogs both loved the climb. It was short enough for Bear to manage easily and steep enough for Shipley to burn off some stamina. Like so many springer spaniels, he had energy to spare, and worked it off by running to the top of the hill, turning and running down at least twice, before moving on to the more pressing business of finding interesting smells.

Max watched Shipley. Now established and trained as an ace sniffer dog, Shipley had a regular appointment at the doctor's surgery. He had an uncanny ability to detect illnesses before any real symptoms had appeared. He'd alerted the doctor to the presence of cancer in two Exham patients who'd called in with vague symptoms of tiredness or inability to sleep, and as a result, Dr Sheffield had overcome his initial scepticism. He'd given instructions to the surgery's receptionist to book similar patients in on Monday afternoons.

'Of course,' Max had pointed out, as he and Libby had discussed it with Dr Sheffield in the rather bleak GP surgery, 'anyone who's offered a Monday appointment will think they have cancer.'

'Better that than missing it,' Dr Sheffield had said in a matter-of-fact voice. He was a good, conscientious and intelligent doctor but lacked the slightest hint of an old-school bedside manner.

Shipley clinics were now a regular feature. An unexpected benefit of the dog's work was that Dr Sheffield's wife, Joanna, who'd taken a while to settle into Exham, had finally found a special niche for herself. She'd begun to volunteer in the Shipley clinic, giving apprehensive patients a chance to talk through their worries, along with endless cups of tea.

'It's killing several birds with one stone,' Max had pointed out. 'Shipley's doing a useful job saving lives instead of digging holes in our flower beds and barking at visitors, people are getting treatment earlier, and Joanna Sheffield's discovered she has a talent for listening, much to everyone's surprise.'

Libby had said, 'She helps even the most distraught patients to relax.' She'd shivered, trying to imagine the terror of thinking you might have cancer. 'And she's thinking of leaving teaching and training as a hypnotherapist. She's wanted to, for years, but her husband used to laugh at her. He said he's a scientist and doesn't believe in mumbo-jumbo. That was before Shipley came along with his skills. Dr Sheffield has a much more open mind, now.'

'Job done, Shipley,' Max said, as the dog arrived, panting, tail wagging, at his feet.

They were approaching the top of the hill and Libby panted a little. 'I wish we could find Mandy's attacker so easily.'

'Let's sit down and think,' Max said. 'It's a beautiful afternoon. Look, you can see the sea over there.'

Somerset spread itself out before them, flaunting its charms. The sea to one side glittered enticingly, and the Levels lay green and verdant, criss-crossed with almost dry rhynes, for apart from a brief shower just after the History Society found the bones, there had been little rain since the downpour that had brought the monk's bones into Washford River.

The M5 buzzed faintly and Max could see a steady stream of

bee-like cars queuing through Somerset, their passengers in a hurry to get to holiday lets in Devon and Cornwall. Max breathed a deep sigh. The passers-through had no idea of the historical treasures they were missing. Somerset was one of England's unsung heroes.

He breathed in the heat of summer, watching a faint haze shimmer above the Levels, as a kestrel hovered over the motorway, head motionless, eyes like lasers, searching out small rodents for lunch.

It was almost midsummer. The hectic excitement of Glastonbury's music festival was over, the enthusiastic regulars had dispersed and throngs of excited teenagers, thrilled with their first visit, had returned home through hours of traffic jams, nursing headaches and bewailing lost possessions, for hot baths in decent bathrooms. Now, the Druids were gearing up for their one day in the spotlight at the summer solstice. Soon, the summer would fade, the evenings draw in and carnival season would begin. Max sighed. The years seemed so short, these days.

'It's like a postcard, isn't it?' Libby said, flopping down beside him and encompassing the view with a wave of her hand. Bear rested by her side. 'It's hard to believe last night even happened. It feels like one of those nightmares that dissolves in daylight.' She ran her hands into Bear's thick fur and rubbed her face on the soft ruff around his neck. 'My head's aching from trying to think things through.'

Max agreed. 'We need to talk to everyone at the ghost hunt. Who was where at the abbey, what we heard, what Mandy's told us – we don't have much yet, but Gemma and Ian took statements. Morrison said he'll give us access to that. We need to be patient for a few days.'

'A few days?' Libby wailed. Bear's ears twitched at the noise. 'Sorry, Bear,' she said.

'It's hard to wait while the police undertake what DCI Morrison calls "proper policing", but we don't want to get in their way,' Max said, slowly. 'But I think you might be right.'

'About what? What did I say?' Libby felt drowsy. The combination of two hours' sleep last night, no appetite and the day's warm sunshine threatened to send her to sleep.

'You wondered if finding the bones had anything to do with the attack.'

'I did. I do. But I can't see how.'

'Nor can I, but we can't sit around for too long, waiting for information from Morrison's team to solve the mystery.'

Libby sat up. 'We should start with the abbey, and work out where everyone was when Mandy was attacked.'

'Good idea,' Max said. 'We'll do that tomorrow. I have an old guide book, with a plan of the buildings, in my study. Now, I suggest we go home, have dinner and get an early night. We'll think better after a decent sleep.'

Next morning, after breakfast, Libby and Max made for his study.

Libby headed for the bookcase. 'One of the things I love about you, Max, is your organisation. If I had a library like this, the books would be all higgledy-piggledy, some lying on their sides, shoved in any old how.'

Max stood next to her. 'You'd have cookery books mixed up with Shakespeare, and coffee-table books on art among all your crime novels. But that's OK. It's the way your mind works, leaping from one thing to another. That's why you solve things. You make connections that wouldn't occur to someone like me, or to your son Robert, for that matter. We think in straight lines.'

Libby's cheeks were warm with pleasure. 'I've never heard anyone describe my mind so generously,' she admitted. 'I always thought I was just bad at concentrating.' She looked along the rows of neatly arranged books, reading the titles, determined to solve the two mysteries. Finding Mandy's attacker was her number one priority, although she longed to know more about the body in the abbey stream.

Max reached past her. 'And, here's a guide book with a plan of the abbey. I knew I had one. I didn't think to take it with me the other evening.'

'Then let's start there,' Libby said. 'We need to see where everyone was when Mandy was attacked. Because it's most likely the attacker was one of the people staying there overnight.'

Max groaned. 'Which means, sad to say, it's most likely it was someone we know.'

Libby bit her lips. 'I don't like it, but I think you're right,' she said. 'In theory, it was possible for someone from outside the ghost hunt to attack Mandy, but the note must have been slipped to her during the evening, when we were the only people there. That narrows it down. So, let's get stuck in.'

Max moved his computer aside and spread the plan of the abbey across his desk. Libby wielded a pencil.

'We were here, in this little room, with Reg,' she said, marking crosses with their initials. 'The room that was once used by the— what was that word?'

'The Corrodian – a rich pensioner living there, looked after by the monks.'

'It was very uncomfortable, sitting against that wall, by the way If I went ghost-spotting again – which I won't, under any circumstances – I'd take one of those chairs Jemima and her friends used. They know a thing or two.'

Max grinned at her, and made a note next to Reg's name. 'He was with us until he went to stretch his legs,' he pointed out. 'What time was that?'

'About ten, I think.' Libby looked up, frowning. 'I glanced at my watch when Reg went out. Was he gone for a long time?'

'At least fifteen minutes. But that was before Ian Smith rang the bell and we all raced into the cloister. Then, you and I both dozed off. We don't know exactly when Mandy was attacked, except that it was after Ian Smith's stupid prank.'

'But not by Reg, surely. Why on earth would he want to hurt her? Their affair was all over years ago.'

Max shook his head. 'Reg is a big guy,' he mused. 'If he hit her, he's likely to do the sort of damage that would easily crack her skull. It could have been him, in theory.'

'He's your friend, Max. Don't you trust him?'

Max walked across the room, and back again. 'I've known Reg for a few years. Our paths crossed when I was tracking down some financial irregularities involving fine art and valuable books, and we've met from time to time, whenever he comes to England. That's not enough to count him out; not yet. But I'd be surprised. I'd have to see plenty of evidence before I believed it was him, and there's nothing as yet. Reg and Mandy had a connection with each other, and he had the opportunity, but so did everyone there.'

They worked through the list of ghost hunters, drawing crosses on the map to show their positions at the beginning of the evening.

'But,' Max said, 'we don't know who stayed together in their groups and who went out and about. We need to talk to everyone.'

Libby said, 'Let's start with Reg. Where's he living while he's in this part of the country?'

'He told me he's staying in an Airbnb in Bristol, and he's longing to be asked round for some of your cooking. He deserves it. He sent us that spectacular wedding present.'

They studied the framed cartoon of them both that hung on the wall.

'I didn't realise my nose was so big,' Max said.

'Bigger,' Libby insisted. 'He was flattering you. But I think he took liberties with my hair. I do comb it, sometimes.'

'He's good, though. Talented. We're recognisable and who

needs flattery?' Max looked away, out to the garden. 'I really hope it's not Reg,' he said.

'Me too.' Libby turned back to the plan. 'Moving on, then. We know Mandy was fine when Ian Smith pulled that stupid trick with his bell. That was around eleven o'clock. To be honest, I was glad he did, because I was about to fall asleep. It's so hard to stay awake when there's nothing happening, isn't it?'

'I did make a suggestion, if you remember, but you refused.'

She grinned, remembering. 'Reg would have come back at the wrong time, you can be sure. It was tempting, though. But I don't know what the monks would have thought. They were strictly celibate.'

Max sat back. 'Supposedly,' he replied. 'It's hard to be sure what they got up to. I've read a couple of books about monasteries in the sixteenth century, and there had been some, er, how shall I put it? Some easing of restrictions.'

'Not to the extent of having women in the Abbey, surely?' Libby gasped.

'Not officially, no.'

'Well,' Libby shook her head, 'human nature's a powerful thing.'

Max was drawing links between the crosses on the map. 'Angela was with Mandy and Steve, until Mandy went off and Steve followed, soon after.'

'You're not thinking he's a suspect, are you? He's nuts about her. They're planning a life together, in London.'

Max chewed his pen, pensively. 'What if he followed her into the gatehouse and saw her with whoever gave her the note?'

'No.' Libby sounded positive.

'You can't decide, "No, it can't possibly be him," for every name,' Max said quietly. 'This is going to be painful enough, because we know so many of the suspects. We need to avoid either accusing or discounting anyone until we know more.'

'Very well, an open mind it is,' Libby said, sounding tetchy. 'I suppose you want to know where I was when you went out to get rid of all the beer, as you put it.'

'See? It could have been you, running quickly out to the gatehouse, or me. I don't think you could have got there, attacked Mandy, and got back before me, but the other day I noticed you had quite a turn of speed when you set off after Shipley.'

'Well, thank you for that vote of confidence.'

'On the other hand,' Max said, reasonable, 'you don't know where I went. No one saw me.'

'Stop it,' Libby pointed a finger at him. 'I know it wasn't you and you know it wasn't me. We can trust each other. I agree with you about everyone else, though. No one will be crossed off the list until we have sufficient evidence.'

Their eyes locked. Libby remembered that when they first met, Max had suspected her of involvement in the shady deal that sent Chesterton Wendlebury to jail. He said, as though reading her mind, 'Even when I was falling head over heels for you, I still had to suspect you. I can't tell you how relieved I was to find you had nothing to do with any of that financial funny business.'

Libby's eyes narrowed. 'Wendlebury,' she said. 'He was with us for a while in the Abbey – and then he left us. Where did he go?'

Max drew a big exclamation mark beside a cross with CW next to it.

Libby said, 'I like him for our suspect. I don't trust him an inch.'

24

Max put a large glass of Libby's favourite red wine into her hand that evening. They'd spent most of the day reading about Cleeve Abbey and its monks. 'Here, you deserve this,' he said, just as a knock at the door set Shipley barking. 'All right,' Max said, and the dog fell silent as he went to open the door. Bear looked up from one of his favourite spots, sprawled in a heap with Fuzzy, on the rug in front of the unlit fire, and watched with sleepy eyes as Max ushered Jemima Bakewell into the room.

'Oh, dear,' she muttered. 'I've disturbed you. I'm so sorry.'

'Not at all,' Max said. 'Let me get you a drink.'

Libby said, 'We're just about to eat, and I've made a casserole with more than enough for three, so I hope you'll join us.'

Jemima fingered the pendant at her throat. 'Well, I didn't mean... It's a bad time, I thought you'd have finished eating. Oh, dear, maybe I'll come back.'

'Nonsense.' Max had already poured another glass of wine. 'Get this down you and join us. Libby's only happy when she's feeding people, and now we're married, I don't count.'

'Well, that's very... I mean, thank you, if you don't mind. It's just...' She took a long swig from her glass. 'Oh, that's nice – Pinot Noir?'

'You know your wine,' Max approved. 'From New Zealand.'

The alcohol was already warming Jemima's cheeks. 'Thank you, I'd love to stay to eat with you. Your food is famous, Libby.'

'And it should be ready right about now, so come into the kitchen. We don't often use the dining room – it's far too grand for Max and me. We need at least half a dozen guests to make it comfortable.'

'Oh, what a lovely room.' Jemima looked around the kitchen. 'A proper range cooker and a Belfast sink – one of my dreams. Of course, there's no room for such luxury in my little terrace in Wells.'

'I only married Max for his old-style kitchen. Mine, in Hope Cottage, is strictly functional for baking. That's where I started my business.'

'And you've done very well,' Jemima said, with an approving nod.

Libby hid a smile. All those years as a Classics teacher in one of Wells' best schools had left its mark on Jemima. She sounded as though she was about to hand Libby a special prize.

'Now,' Max said, once they were seated around the scrubbed kitchen table, tucking into plates brimming with beef in red wine, 'how can we help, Jemima?'

She gave a girlish giggle. Libby smiled. Max's blue eyes often provoked that kind of behaviour in single women of a certain age. 'I almost forgot why I came, I've been enjoying myself so much,' Jemima said. She laid her knife and fork together on her plate, suddenly serious. 'You see, I'm sure you two will be helping the police find the person who attacked poor Mandy. I can't get her out of my mind. Such an original young woman, isn't she? I knew one or two girls like her when I was teaching – they liven everything up, when they're around.'

Her eyes glistened and a lump formed in Libby's throat. She swallowed, hard.

Jemima was still talking. 'I thought I should tell you what I saw that night. I don't know if it's important, but, Libby, you once told me that nothing was unimportant, and I'm sure that's true.'

She took another mouthful of wine. Libby wanted to hurry her but knew she should let her use her own words.

At last, Jemima said, 'I was sitting with Quentin and Archie, talking about the abbey and laughing a little at the very idea of ghosts. Such nonsense, I've always thought, although I've a feeling Quentin was almost hoping to see something.' She gave a short chuckle. 'He's not a real historian, you know. Not like Archie – I mean, Dr Phillips. Quentin dabbles.' Her eyes glowed.

Libby raised an eyebrow. Which of her two gentlemen admirers was Jemima contemplating with such pleasure?

'Then, I looked out of the window,' Jemima continued. 'We were upstairs in the monks' old dormitory – such an interesting place, with all the alcoves for the monks' beds, you can really imagine them sleeping there every night... well...' She met Max's gaze.

One of his eyebrows was raised. Libby guessed he was thinking the monks might have been getting up to more than sleeping.

Jemima blushed. Her mind seemed to be running along the same tracks. 'That's irrelevant, anyway,' she said. 'The point is,' she half-rose from her seat, waving a finger in her enthusiasm, 'I saw something.'

Libby closed her eyes for a second. Was Jemima ever going to get to the point?

Max nodded, patiently. 'Go on,' he said. 'What did you see?'

'I saw a monk, that's what I saw.' She peered from one face to the other. 'Now, you're thinking what a foolish old bat I am, imagining things, probably had too much to drink – and it's true, Archie did keep offering me tiny little swigs from his flask – but I can assure you, the sight I saw turned me stone-cold sober in an instant. You see, I saw a monk walking around the corner, across the remains of the old chapel.' She stared at Libby, eyes wide. 'Possibly on his way to the gatehouse.'

Libby gulped. 'A monk? You saw a monk walking towards the gatehouse?'

'He glided along, as though his feet were hardly touching the ground. It gave me the shivers. I called the others across to look, but they thought I was joking at first, and by the time they came over, the monk had gone.' Jemima finished eating and sat back with a sigh of satisfaction. 'Lovely stew, Libby, just lovely.' She patted her stomach. 'Of course, when we found Mandy had been attacked, it came to me that what I'd seen perhaps wasn't a monk at all.' Her voice rose dramatically. 'I believe I saw the attacker.' She dropped her voice again, sounding a little disappointed. 'Although, he did look like a monk, with a hood pulled up around his head.'

Max glanced up. 'A hood? Are you sure? Mandy was wearing a cloak, so you might have seen her.'

Jemima shook her head. 'I'm quite positive. There was a hood. My eyesight is excellent, when I'm wearing my glasses. It was dark, of course, but the stars were out – there was definitely enough light to make out the shape of a hood.'

Max was tracing patterns on the table with a spoon. 'Jemima, thank you so much. I think you've given us the best clue yet.'

Two heads swivelled his way.

'You see, we all had big coats with us, and several of us were wearing sweatshirts with hoods.'

Jemima nodded agreement. 'Everyone seems to have them, these days. They call them hoodies, I believe.'

Max went on, 'We were all prepared to be cold that night, even though it was summer. We know our climate well enough to wrap up warm, even in June. So, if someone went out, pulling their hood up and wearing a coat, it would be easy to mistake them for a monk.'

'Especially,' Libby added with a smile, 'if you'd had a drink or two from Archie's flask.'

'Exactly.' Jemima sounded triumphant. 'So, there's a nice big clue for the two of you to work on.'

Libby said, 'Do you know what time you saw the, er, person?'

Jemima beamed. 'Indeed, I do. It was almost exactly twelve fifteen. I looked at my watch, because I wanted to make a note of it for Rosalind. Such a nice woman,' she added, vaguely. 'If a little bossy. But now I must go, because it's time for me to feed my cat. I took him in from Mrs Marchant, the cat lady in Wells.'

Still talking, refusing to stay for dessert, Jemima backed herself out of Exham House.

'Should she be driving?' Libby asked.

Max shrugged. 'I didn't give her much to drink; the glass was very small. I think she'll be fine. But what about her story?'

'It sounds as though she got a real glimpse of the attacker. What time did she say she saw him?'

'She looked at her watch at twelve fifteen, she said. So, that gives us a nice timeline for the attack.'

'Unfortunately, several of us were wearing sweaters with

hoods, that night,' Libby said. 'And, if I were the killer, I'd have got rid of the hoodie at the earliest opportunity.'

She looked at Max, disappointed. Of course, the attacker would have disposed of his incriminating clothes, even if he had no idea anyone had spotted him. 'Still, knowing the time helps. We can find out where people were at that time.' She took a last mouthful of wine. 'I think we should talk to Rosalind. She had that clipboard, and she came to see us all in our positions, giving directions about what we should all be doing. I bet she made loads of notes. Maybe she even saw the mysterious monk herself.' Libby's hand flew to her mouth. 'Oh dear. I've had a thought. Do you think Jemima's in any danger? She says she didn't tell the police, because Archie and Quentin didn't see it and they can't back her up, and she's afraid the police will think she's making it up.'

'Why should they? She's a perfectly respectable lady.'

Libby shook her head. 'She is, but I think Jemima's used to being a bit of a laughing stock. You know, ageing spinster ex-schoolmistress with no partner or close relatives. I bet she used to get hassle from the kids at school – probably still does from local kids. No wonder she's nervous about making herself a target for ridicule.'

Max said. 'Why don't you ring her tomorrow morning, tell her to take care and encourage her to talk to the police.'

'Let's just hope it's Gemma she talks to, not Ian Smith.'

'It feels like old times, doesn't it?' Max said, as he arrived with Libby at the police station. 'We've been here a few times, now.'

She grumbled. 'I never quite feel comfortable. Every time I leave here, I breathe this big sigh of relief that the police haven't found out some crime I once committed and forgot all about. Like, a library book I never returned.'

Max opened the door. 'Ah, the old guilty conscience. Glad to see it plagues you, too.'

'Surely you never did anything against the law?'

Max grinned. 'Don't tell DCI Morrison, but I once shoplifted a bar of chocolate. But since I ate the evidence, I think I'm safe enough. Funny thing, though. It made me feel sick, and I've never really liked chocolate in the same way – apart from yours,' he added, hastily. 'I mean bars, like Cadbury's and KitKats—'

'I know what you mean. And I don't mind at all that you don't like chocolate. It leaves more for me. And Mandy.' She clutched at his hand. 'Angela says she's still not conscious.'

'I'm sure it'll get better. It's early days.'

'I suppose so.' Libby sounded less than confident.

Max was pleased when DC Gemma greeted them at the station. 'The DCI said Ian and I could talk to you,' she grinned. 'The boss himself is off to a meeting, something about forward planning, so he's leaving it to us.'

They followed her along the dull, grey-painted, institutional corridor, into a large open-plan room full of desks and computers. Max nodded at a couple of police officers he recognised from previous jobs he'd worked on.

'I've booked a room,' Gemma said, ushering them into a miniscule, glass-walled pod. She was, Max realised, pink with pleasure at being charged with talking to them and reporting back directly to the DCI.

PC Ian Smith arrived, his stomach almost bursting out of his shirt. 'Come on then. Let's get this over.' He'd long stopped trying to cover his jealous dislike of Libby and Max. 'Morrison's called in the brains trust, I see. Can't leave it to us lesser mortals.' He flopped into a chair, legs stuck out in front. 'Get us a cup of coffee, would you, love?' he said to Gemma.

The glare she gave him would have frozen a more sensitive man into silence.

He laughed, nastily. 'Can't even suggest coffee without being accused of sexism, these days, can you, Ramshore?'

'We're fine, thanks,' Libby put in, with a glance at Gemma. 'We hoped we could pick your brains about Mandy's attack.'

Gemma sighed. 'Poor Mandy. You know, I love policing, but when it involves someone you know – like Mandy – well, all we can do is our best, I suppose. Find the culprit as fast as possible and bring them to justice.' Her frown lifted. 'I expect you know she's still unconscious, and not able to answer questions yet, but the doctors are very hopeful she'll wake soon. At least, to look on the bright side, it's not a murder enquiry.'

Libby shivered. 'And it could have been, very easily.'

'But that means, I suppose,' Max said, 'there's less police time for it?'

Ian Smith snorted. 'No time for anything, these days. Except chasing up non-criminal racist behaviour. Waste of effort, that is.'

Max wondered how much longer DCI Morrison would put up with Smith's behaviour. One day, the man would go too far. That day couldn't come soon enough.

As they ran through the events at the abbey, Max realised the police knew little more than he and Libby. He showed Gemma their plan of the abbey, with the whereabouts of the ghost-watchers marked by crosses and notes.

Ian Smith jabbed at the cloister with a grubby finger. 'You were all there after I rang the bell, so that helps with the time-line.' He grinned. 'I bet you thought I was just playing silly beggars. On the contrary, it was policing at its finest. Checking you all out without having to find my way in the dark to all the corners you'd chosen. Pretty clever wheeze, wasn't it? That Rosalind woman wasn't amused, though. Said I'd stop the monks' spirits from appearing. Stupid woman. As if there were ghosts. Who believes that nonsense, anyway?'

Max took a long look at Ian Smith, wondering whether to change his assessment of the constable's abilities. Perhaps he wasn't quite so stupid as he appeared.

'You counted everyone?' Libby asked.

Smith nodded. 'Even the old codgers from the dormitory. Once they'd made it down the stairs.' He sniggered.

'Why were you both there, that night?' Max asked. 'Was it official policing?

Gemma smiled. 'Undercover. Well, not really undercover, I suppose, because everyone knew who we were and we showed our warrants, but the truth is the boss—'

'DCI Morrison?'

'That's right. He suggested I might be interested in going along, seeing if there was anything in it for the police to look at. He said the Exham History Society had been at the centre of so much crime in the county that he wanted us to take a closer look, see if there's anything strange going on with these bones.'

Libby spoke up. 'You're talking about Chesterton Wendlebury, aren't you?'

Gemma nodded. 'We thought it was strange that he appeared on the scene just when the bones were found. Did he have anything to do with them? He's living in his cousin's nearby Manor House, so it might just be coincidence, but the boss wanted us to find out more about this monk, see if there are any possible links with Wendlebury, and the ghost hunt seemed like a perfect opportunity. Also, he knows I've worked with you and Max before. Of course, I jumped at the chance, and finding Chesterton Wendlebury at the abbey confirmed my bad feeling. He's like one of those factory owners from the war – you know, the ones who sat back and took government money for making munitions for the war effort, while the ordinary people did the work.'

Max and Libby both chuckled. 'That's a perfect description,' Libby said. 'He simply oozes sleaze.'

Gemma screwed up her nose. 'What a disgusting thought. Anyway, I loved the idea of joining the ghost hunt, quite frankly, and so did Ian, even though it was semi-official and unpaid. I sometimes suspect the boss likes us to do a spot of unofficial policing, where possible. He thinks we can prevent crime before it happens, by keeping our fingers on the local pulse. It gets him into bother, sometimes, with the higher-ups and their priorities, budgets and so on. I think that's why he's been summoned today, although don't tell anyone I told you that.'

Libby was frowning. 'How did DCI Morrison know Chesterton Wendlebury would be at the ghost hunt? We didn't.'

Gemma grinned. 'I told the boss about Wendlebury arriving while you were all looking at the monk's bones. Apparently, he's living at Priory Manor, looking after the estate for his cousin, who has all kinds of plans for making money out of it.' She tapped a finger against her nose. 'The Wendleburys are after a quick profit. As we know, that's what got Chesterton into trouble in the first place. Anyway, the boss did his kind of "nod and wink" act, complete with sighing and groaning. You know how he does. Then he suggested the two of us should go along to the ghost hunt and find out more.'

Max stored that piece of information away, to think about later. Apart from telling him the police had their eyes on Chesterton Wendlebury, it suggested two other possibilities. One was that DCI Morrison's approach, encouraging his teams to think beyond their immediate remit, might be under pressure. How secure was his job? If his enlightened approach to policing changed, Libby and Max might find it more difficult to work with the police. Libby had encountered several police stone walls when she first moved to Exham and a different DCI had been in charge.

The other conclusion Max drew from Gemma's remarks was that Morrison had singled the young detective constable out, possibly seeing her as a likely promotion prospect in the future. There was a gap at detective sergeant level, since Max's son, Joe, had moved on, replaced by a series of other officers who'd also moved out to other teams. Perhaps Gemma would be in line for promotion, soon. And that, Max was sure, would be well deserved.

Jemima rang, later that day, excited. 'I believe we have a clue for you,' she said, 'about Bernard, our monk. You see, Archie – I mean, Dr Phillips.' Libby imagined Jemima's blush. 'He wants to show us something else he found in his archives.'

Sure enough, when Libby and Max arrived, Archie's ancient Ford Focus was parked outside Jemima's house.

Libby wagged a finger at Shipley. 'Now, you leave Dr Phillips alone.'

Max took the spaniel's lead. 'He'll have to learn to love dogs if he has designs on Jemima. She's crazy about Bear. She insisted we couldn't come without him.'

'Bear isn't the problem,' Libby said. 'Archie's used to him. It's Shipley's bounce that bothers him.'

Max spoke sternly to the spaniel. 'Today's your chance to show him you can behave. Pretend it's Monday. You're wonderful at the surgery.'

Libby said, 'I think good behaviour for one day exhausts him, like a child starting school. He uses up more energy sitting quietly than he does racing around the fields.'

Shipley must have been listening, she decided, as Jemima ushered them into her house, for he sat obediently next to Bear, at Jemima's feet – the handful of dog biscuits Libby passed to Jemima also helped.

A large, leather-bound book lay open on Jemima's circular dining table.

'This isn't the original, of course – that's far too valuable to bring out of the library,' Archie explained. 'It's a copy of an illuminated manuscript, rescued from a few books that found their way from Cleeve Abbey, when it was dissolved, to Wells Cathedral library. We suspect some of the monks smuggled them out for safe keeping.' Archie smoothed his hand over the page.

Everyone leaned forward to get a better look. The top half of the page was filled by the drawing of a monk, giving Communion. He held in one hand a golden goblet, raising it towards the crucifix just above the altar.

Libby nodded, trying to look intelligent. 'I've seen this kind of illumination before. It's very beautiful, but I don't quite—'

Archie pointed to the writing on the page. 'I can't really translate it all myself, or at least, not without several hours of work, but there are a few words at the bottom of the page that are simpler. They say, *furati est.*'

'Sorry?' Max said.

Jemima grinned. 'It says, in Latin of course, that something was stolen.'

'Well done,' Archie beamed. 'So useful to have a classics teacher around.' Jemima gave her girlish giggle as he went on, 'The monks always wrote in Latin. Actually, most of them just copied and didn't always understand all the words themselves, but sometimes they made a note on the page. Their comments can be quite amusing.' He looked over the top of his reading glasses at Libby and Max. 'You sometimes find the Latin for things like, "Now this work is done, I need a drink."'

Libby chuckled. 'Really?'.

He nodded. 'That's from a different manuscript. This one tells us about a theft, but unfortunately, not what property was stolen.' Archie rubbed his chin. 'We can make some informed guesses. We know Henry VIII took – stole – everything from the monasteries and sold it on for a profit. He was a greedy man, and a profligate one. In short, he was broke. He needed money. Closing the monasteries served a dual purpose of filling his coffers and removing Roman Catholic influence from England.'

'So, how does that link to our monk, Bernard?'

'We think he may have been working on this book.' Archie pointed at the picture. 'Look at the crucifix.'

They all nodded, slightly puzzled.

He turned to the guidebook. 'It's in the guidebook from Cleeve Abbey – the crucifix is the one carved above the gatehouse.'

Jemima said, 'So, one of the Cleeve monks thought there was a theft from the abbey?'

'More than just Henry VIII's theft of treasures, I'm sure. And it was most likely our monk, Bernard, as he was the abbey scribe. There were only thirteen monks there at the time.'

Archie was tugging at his ear. 'How many monks in a small monastery like this would be working on the illuminations? Not more than one or two, I'll bet. Our monk has blue stains on his teeth, so he must have devoted many hours to his work. Let's assume he wanted to pass on a clue. We don't know who he thought might read it. He might have meant it for one of the other monks. They were silent, in this abbey. That was part of being a Cistercian. They were very strict about that. Or, he might have been afraid of someone, and unwilling to say that he knew about some theft or other.' He stopped talking. 'I don't see what else this tells us, though. It's a dead end.'

Libby said, 'Not really. Don't forget how Bernard died. That hole in his head was probably inflicted deliberately, our university researchers say. And, if that's the case, we need to consider why someone would want to kill him.'

Jemima was on her feet, bouncing with excitement. 'Because he knew they'd stolen something, of course. I think it's obvious. Bernard was murdered because he knew too much. Isn't that thrilling? A murder mystery to solve, from all those years ago. Oh...' She stopped talking and her face fell. 'Oh dear. Do you know, for a moment I was so engrossed in the medieval monastery that I quite forgot about Mandy.'

'Yes,' Libby said, her stomach suddenly tied in knots. 'So did I, just for a minute. And even if we're right, and we're making huge assumptions, I don't see how there can possibly be any link between a theft and murder all those years ago and Mandy's attacker.'

'Well,' Max said, 'we can't see a link just yet, but that doesn't mean there isn't one. We've made a great deal of progress, thanks to you, Archie, and we can't stop now. We must keep looking until we find the answers to both crimes.'

28

Next morning, Libby's stomach was, once again in knots, but this time it was excitement, not dread, making her heart beat faster, for her son Robert and his heavily pregnant wife Sarah were spending the day at Exham House.

'The baby's due in about three weeks,' Sarah said, leaning back against the cushions in the comfiest sofa in Exham House. 'I've lost the ability to do anything except think about him. The nursery's ready now. Robert spent hours building cupboards, I've been painting and Ali came over the other day with some wonderful curtains she'd made. We decided on lemon and green. We don't want a little boy's bedroom.'

'Did Ali help choose the colour scheme?' Libby laughed. 'It's very Brazilian.'

Robert, earnest as always, nodded. 'I can't wait for the little fellow to meet his auntie.'

With parents-in-waiting in the house, Libby managed to push away, just for a few hours, the terrible memory of the ill-fated ghost hunt and the anxiety of Mandy's head injury. The day

passed in a pleasant haze of arguing over names and arrangements for the birth, until Robert took a sleepy Sarah home.

Libby had the first full night's sleep she'd managed since the
ghost hunt.

Angela phoned the next morning, at breakfast time. Mandy
had regained consciousness. 'She opened her eyes last night for a
few minutes,' Angela said. 'That was all, but we're hoping she'll
be awake for longer today.'

'That's wonderful news.'

Angela took a second before answering. 'Ye-es,' she said. 'It is,
but—'

Libby swallowed. Why was Angela sounding so guarded?

'You see, she couldn't say anything. At least, nothing we could
understand. She just muttered something to Steve that sounded
like gobbledegook.'

Libby, horrified, clutched the phone, her knuckles white. 'I
expect she was just too tired.'

'Probably.' Even over the phone, Libby could tell Angela was
making a huge effort to sound positive. She went on, 'She's been
unconscious for a few days so she's bound to be confused. She'll
be better today, I'm sure.'

Libby couldn't concentrate after that phone call. Too many
dreadful possibilities chased each other through her mind. She
set to work baking, hand-kneading until her muscles ached, but,
for once, the task had no therapeutic effect. She kept picturing
Mandy, lying in hospital, unable to talk.

She realised Max was talking to her. 'You've been beating that
dough for almost half an hour. I'm sure you've hammered it into
submission.'

Libby made an effort, but her smile wobbled. 'It's Mandy.'

'I know.' Max lifted the dough from the table and dumped it
into a bowl. 'There, that can look after itself for now. Come and

sit down. The French windows are open in the study, the sun's shining and the dogs are full of beans. They'll cheer you up.'

Silently, Libby followed him into his study. They'd brought in new rugs and a couple of fluffy cushions since Libby arrived, but still it had the slight feel of a nineteenth-century men's club, with bookshelves ranging the full length of two walls. Only the state-of-the-art computer on the desk that faced the garden, Libby's wedding present to Max, challenged the room's old-world ambience.

'Now, sit down and drink this coffee,' Max insisted.

She took a sip. 'Mm. Nice. Did you add something?'

'Tiny drop of whisky.'

'Tiny?' At least Max could still make Libby laugh, despite her worry.

'Tell me what you're thinking,' Max said. 'I thought you'd be relieved that Mandy's awake. You could probably visit soon.'

'Of course I'm relieved she's getting better,' Libby said. 'But Mandy, not talking? Can you even imagine that?'

'Not really, but recovery from a blow on the head can take a while. You have to be patient.'

Libby drew a long, shaky breath. 'That's the point, though. How long? A week? A month? Forever? I mean, you hear of people paralysed after a blow on the head.'

'But the doctors haven't suggested that, have they?'

'No, I suppose not. It's the not talking that scares me. What if she can never tell us what happened to her at the abbey? What if she never talks again, about anything?'

Max had turned his head away. Libby knew he was trying to hide his own worry. 'We'll have to be patient. Wait and see.'

Libby said, 'The vicar, Amy Fisher – remember her, from Watchet?' He nodded, and she went on, 'She's going to talk about Mandy in her church.'

'I think everyone in Exham – in the whole of Somerset – will be wishing her well.'

Libby shivered. 'Except for whoever hit her on the head. They tried to kill her, Max, and so far we've no idea why.'

He nodded. 'I'll call DCI Morrison again, find out if there's any news. We're still on his books, as preferred consultants.'

'Civilian officers, you mean,' Libby managed a smile.

'Whatever he calls us, we don't get paid much,' Max pointed out. 'But he'll tell us what he knows. He trusts us. And we're fully vetted.'

Libby got to her feet. 'I've been trying to keep my mind off Mandy, waiting until she woke up, expecting she'll be able to tell us what happened. But I can't bear it any longer. Someone's walking about, scot-free, after attacking our friend and it's time we found out who.'

'And,' Max put in, 'why? Why would someone attack Mandy, of all people? She wouldn't hurt a fly.'

Libby shrugged. 'Something she knows? After all, she went to meet someone. Who could it have been? And did it have anything to do with Bernard, the murdered monk?'

Max nodded, thoughtfully. 'I think a visit to Rosalind is over-due. She knows about historical buildings, and she was at Cleeve Abbey that night. According to Gemma, neither her statement nor the notes she took at the ghost hunt gave any clues, but a friendly visit from us might jog her memory.'

'What do we know about Rosalind Thurston?' Max asked, as he drove with Libby and the dogs, who grunted happily in the back of the Land Rover, along the road that hugged the north coast of Somerset. 'You spent hours this morning nosing into her background.'

'Well, you're the one who showed me how much you can find out from Facebook, Twitter and so on. I've even mastered Instagram. It's full of photos of my cakes and chocolates, these days. Can't seem to understand TikTok, though.'

'No one over forty can.'

'Anyway,' Libby continued, 'as we know from our phone call with Rosalind, she lives in Porlock, which is a lovely little town, apart from its ridiculously steep road. Her garden looks out over the bay. All terraced flower beds and Mediterranean herbs. Had a visit from a *Gardener's World* presenter, once.'

'Husband? Children?' Max prompted.

'Husband in residence, children grown up and left home, a boy at university and a girl married and living in Scotland.' Libby ticked them off on her fingers. 'Rosalind retired from a job as the finance director of some non-governmental organisation. Which means,' she added, 'they get money from the government to do something worthwhile. Something to do with training the social care workforce, in this case.'

'Financial director, eh?'

'Yes, I thought you'd like that. The two of you can bond over a spreadsheet or two.'

'It's a bit of a leap from finance to chasing ghosts. Do you think she's having a midlife crisis?'

'You can ask her.'

Max had no time to reply, as a tractor loomed into view ahead with a line of four cars in low gears following it up a hill, and he slowed to join the queue. 'This is what I love about the A39,' he said. 'You never know how long it will take to drive to Minehead, never mind Porlock. It adds a touch of the unknown to every journey.'

Libby looked at her watch. 'I hope Rosalind sees it that way. We're already late. I'd better send a text before she puts the kettle on.'

Bear yawned loudly behind her.

Max said, 'Are you sure she's OK with us bringing the dogs?'

'She insisted. She has a pair of Labradors, herself.'

'Let's hope they all get on, that's all I can say. We can do without a dog fight.'

Finally, the tractor pulled over into a layby to let the cars through, and soon Libby and Max drew up outside Rosalind's thatched cottage.

Max whistled. 'Talk about chocolate boxes.'

'Pretty, isn't it?'

He shook his head as they scrambled from the car. 'Expensive to repair that roof. And isn't it a fire risk?'

'Nonsense. It's as good as any other roof. Just more photogenic.'

Max grunted. 'The windows are too small,' he objected. 'I bet it's dark inside.'

'Stop it, you grumpy old man,' Libby said. 'Here's Rosalind.'

The ghost-hunter had flung her front door wide open and welcomed the visitors like long-lost friends. 'And your dogs are beautiful. Come through, we'll let them out into the garden with my two.' She called, in a piercing voice, 'Conan! Sherlock!'

Max and Libby exchanged a glance as they followed Rosalind through the house.

'Mind your head,' she warned Max. 'The ceilings are low.'

Finally, they emerged into a sunlit garden that took Libby's breath away. A wrought-iron table and chairs occupied a small, circular paved area shaded by an ancient oak tree and surrounded by a profusion of roses in full bloom. Honeysuckle crept over trellises, mingling with late clematis. Paths led, twisting and turning, down the terraced slope in a riot of summer colour, but the star of the show was the sea, sparkling in the sun, reflecting a light so bright that Libby needed sunglasses to fend off the glare.

'This is lovely,' Libby said.

'Isn't it? I can't take the credit, I'm afraid,' Rosalind replied in her cut-glass voice. 'It's all my husband's doing. If Alistair's not at work, he's out in the garden, pruning and digging. I don't have much to do with it, really.'

'It all blends into the view of the sea,' Libby noted. 'And the colours are wonderful. Look at the way those bright red poppies sing out against the silver leaves. I don't know much about gardens, but I think yours is lovely.'

Rosalind laughed. 'It's down to chance, as much as anything. Alistair's terrible with colour. He plants things randomly, says they all look the same colour to him, even the roses, his pride and joy. But then, nature is random, isn't it? He gets away with it. I never interfere out here – he gets annoyed. He's working, today, so you won't meet him, I'm afraid.'

A touch of –what? – sarcasm in her voice surprised Libby. Was this a case of a married couple living two separate lives? Perhaps that was why Rosalind had turned to ghost-hunting, once her children were gone and she'd retired from her high-powered job. Boredom had a lot to answer for.

As the dogs sniffed each other warily, Rosalind poured tea and offered cake. 'It's nothing like your creations, I'm afraid,' she apologised, pushing a strand of her bright hair behind one ear.

Max laughed. 'Everyone says that to Libby.'

'But, to be honest, there's nothing I like more than a cake that someone else has made,' Libby confessed. 'This one looks delicious. It smells great, too.'

'Nonsense,' Rosalind giggled, seeming positively girlish now she was relaxed and at home. Maybe the pushy confidence she'd shown at the abbey had been an act. 'It's just an old Dundee I threw together.'

They chewed the cake politely while Rosalind asked about Mandy.

'Such an, er, original girl, isn't she? All those black clothes in midsummer. So gloomy.'

Libby could almost swear Rosalind gave a little disapproving sniff. 'Mandy's one of the nicest, brightest girls I know,' she said. 'I can't imagine why anyone would want to hurt her.'

'Oh, well, of course not.' Rosalind blinked rapidly. 'I just meant...'

Max put in, 'She's doing well, though. Sitting up and taking notice. I'm sure she'll be fighting fit soon and able to talk to the police.'

Libby, surprised, quickly gained control of her face. Suggesting Mandy was likely to remember what happened was a clever idea.

'Oh, excellent news. Excellent,' Rosalind gushed. 'Does she remember who attacked her?' The teapot in her hand clinked against a cup as she poured each of them a second cup of Earl Grey.

Libby said, 'She can't remember everything that happened.'

'I believe that often happens,' Rosalind said. 'Shock, I suppose.'

Max said, 'We wondered if you noticed anything that night that might help. I know you gave a statement to the police, as we all did, but maybe, since then, you've remembered something. Any clues.'

'If only I could think of something,' Rosalind said, sitting forward on the edge of her chair. 'But I was so busy concentrating on the event,' she gave a little emphasis to the word 'event' and Libby could see how much it had meant to her. 'You see, I'm excited about this ghost-hunting – or paranormal investigation, as we prefer to call it. It's fascinating, you know. People don't believe in it. They're so quick to scoff. But if you look around, there are many examples of evidence that a place can retain something from the people who live there. It's not,' she said severely, glaring at Max in particular, 'just about seeing ghosts. There are sounds, temperature changes, touches on the shoulder, objects shifting position. So many types of evidence and we almost saw something. If only we hadn't been interrupted in the refectory—'

'When Mandy was hurt.'

'Well, yes.' She had the grace to look uncomfortable. 'I don't mean to complain, of course. Very sad. Very sad indeed. I'm just so glad she's getting better.'

Libby, fighting dislike for this strange, ghost-obsessed woman, said, 'We'd like to see any notes you took that night. And any photographs, or sound recordings.'

'I gave my notes to the police, but I kept a copy. Give me a moment and I'll bring them out.'

Rosalind returned, clutching a bulky folder to her chest. Libby helped her to move all the cups and plates onto a tray and Max took it inside the house.

'Kitchen's on the right,' Rosalind called, as she laid the folder on the wrought-iron table and opened it out.

Libby gasped. 'All these notes, from that one night?' she asked.

'I'm very thorough,' Rosalind smiled. 'Obsessed, Alistair calls it.' Her lips clamped tightly together. So, Libby was right. There was tension between these two, despite the charming garden and enviable house.

Libby bent over to look more closely. Rosalind had made notes on a plan of the abbey grounds, as Libby and Max had done. She'd noted where she'd left recording equipment and remotely operated cameras, and the plan was accompanied by page after page of closely written notes.

'I haven't typed these up, yet. I make a few notes on my iPhone, but I find it quicker to write on the clipboard. In the heat of the moment, you know.'

'Well,' Libby said, 'these are certainly meticulous. It will take a while to go through them. Could you possibly let us have copies?'

'Of course. This folder is for you. I photocopied it all after we spoke on the telephone.'

Max returned and leaned over Libby's shoulder, screwing up his eyes to make out the writing. Bear, tiring of the boisterous play of the younger dogs, appeared at his side. 'We should get on our way. We don't want to keep you too long, Rosalind, but thank you so much for all this detail.'

Rosalind's carefully made-up face fell a little. 'Must you go so soon?'

Libby opened her mouth to ask for a tour around the garden, but Max said, 'I'm afraid so. You've been immensely helpful. Thank you so much.'

Slightly puzzled, Libby called for Shipley. His muddy nose suggested he'd been digging in Alistair Thurston's treasured garden, so she delayed no longer but led the way back to the car while Max charmed Rosalind with his thanks and promises to keep in touch.

As he started the engine, she said, 'Why on earth did we have to leave in such a hurry? I was hoping for more tea and possibly a glass of wine or two.'

'I can't keep Shipley under control for a moment longer. He'd dug a hole right under one of those enormous rose bushes and I wanted to get away before Rosalind noticed.'

Libby and Max arrived back at Exham House late that afternoon. Max said, 'I'd better take the dogs out for a run. Their good behaviour was stretched to the limit at Rosalind's house.'

'While you're out, I'll start going through her notes from the ghost hunt. I think they'll keep us going for the rest of the day.'

'She's certainly thorough. Will you be OK on your own?'

'Of course. And Fuzzy will keep me company.' The marmalade cat was lying stretched out on her back in a patch of sun on the carpet in Max's study. 'I think she enjoyed having the house to herself, even though she's very fond of Bear and she's got Shipley under control.' When Libby moved in, Fuzzy had spent several days jumping out at the springer spaniel, and hissing at him from the top of bookshelves, until he learned not to be too ditsy around her. 'She'll warn me if a ghost is about to leap out at me.'

'Very funny. Don't go imagining things. There are no ghosts here since I updated the heating,' Max noted. 'On second thoughts,' he added, clipping on Shipley's lead, 'I'll leave Bear with you. Shipley deserves a real workout and Bear doesn't have so much energy these days.'

Libby raised her eyebrows. 'He can stay to help Fuzzy defend me, then. Come here, old fellow.'

Bear rose, yawned and made his way across the room to sit at her side, resting his head on her knee, looking into her face with melting brown eyes.

'He's such a lovely boy,' she said. 'He cheers me up— Oh!'

'What is it?' Max asked.

'It's an idea – I wonder if it's possible.'

'Come on, spit it out,' Max said, almost out of the door. 'Don't keep me in suspense.'

'It might sound silly, but I wonder if I could take Bear to the hospital with me, when I go to see Mandy. I'm sure he'd help her feel better. What do you think?'

'I think you're a genius. It certainly can't do any harm if the nurses or whatever will let you. Just seeing him walk into a room would lower anyone's blood pressure. We'll look into it. But now I really must take this creature out before he pulls me over.'

On his return to Exham House after his walk with Shipley, Max found Libby kneeling on a dining-room chair at the long, oval walnut table he'd bought when he retired from his original banking job. That seemed so long ago. He'd stayed in financial services, uncovering fraud on behalf of the UK government.

He drew up a chair and leaned over the table beside Libby, his mind refreshed by the walk. He studied Rosalind's notes as meticulously as he had always examined business accounts, searching for inconsistencies and mistakes.

Libby said, 'I'll let you take over. Rosalind has made a note of every footstep she heard, every sigh and cough. It's exhausting to read. My eyes are beginning to water. There's also this.' She held up a SIM card Rosalind had left in a plastic bag, attached to the inside cover of the file. 'Recordings from the whole time we were there. Hours of it, and she hasn't transcribed it, yet.'

'Any visuals?' Max asked.

'Another bag with a memory stick. I attached it to my iPad and had a quick look through, but there's almost nothing to see. A glimpse of someone's light-coloured shirt here, the flash of a torch there. There are a couple of more interesting things, flashes of light which I remember she called "orbs".' Libby pointed to a photograph. 'Rosalind noted them down as possible traces of electromagnetic activity and signs there may be paranormal activity.'

'Or they could be tiny specks of dust caught in the light of a torch?'

'Exactly. There's so much material here, but no record of anyone seeing an actual ghost in a white robe, I'm sorry to say.'

Max ran his eye over the pages in the file. 'She noted down the times she saw people moving around. Look, this is when Reg left us to stretch his legs at 10.05 p.m., according to Rosalind. Then, there's a lot of rather tetchy notes about Ian's bell-ringing trick. But,' he flipped quickly through the pages, 'there's no record of any sighting of Mandy going out to the gatehouse, or of anyone following her. That's odd, isn't it? What was Rosalind doing at...' he consulted the notes he and Libby had made on the plan, 'at around twelve fifteen, when Jemima saw her monk?'

'I expect she'd fallen asleep. I know I was dozing.' Libby yawned. 'Do you realise, we've been at this for hours, and we haven't even eaten dinner. It's almost ten o'clock. I'll get one of my curries out of the freezer and microwave it.'

As she left for the kitchen, the doorbell rang.

'I'll get it,' Max called. He opened the door and gasped. 'Good heavens, man. Whatever's the matter?'

31

REG

Libby dropped the forks back in their drawer and ran out of the kitchen to find Reg just inside the front door.

'Sorry. It's late, isn't it? I wasn't thinking,' he said.

Max was frowning. 'You look terrible. What's happened?'

Reg, usually so calm – unflappable, really – was hunched into his light jacket, the collar tucked half in and half out. 'My whole day sucked, Max. I could do with a drink.'

Libby took his jacket, while Max marched him into the study. 'Here, you look as though you need it.' He handed Reg a half-full glass of whisky. 'Sit down and tell us what's happened.'

Reg slumped into a chair, his long limbs spread like spiders' legs across the floor. Bear came, sensing distress, and laid his head on Reg's lap. 'I just spent three hours in the police station,' Reg began. 'It seems I'm the prime suspect in the attack on Mandy. I thought they were going to lock me up and throw away the key. I didn't think I'd get out without a beating.'

Libby looked blankly at Max. 'A beating?' she said. 'Don't be ridiculous. Why would they?'

Reg snorted. 'Look at me, Libby. A black guy, suspected of attacking a white girl?'

'But that's nonsense. This is Somerset. I mean, why would you think the police would do that?'

Reg took a gulp of whisky, and coughed. 'That's good whisky, Max. I knew I could rely on you.' He sat back, as though slowly relaxing. 'I guess I panicked and overreacted. I forgot I'm in this little out-of-the-way spot in the English countryside where you have coppers on the beat and ask them the time.'

'Not exactly, not any more,' Max put in. 'I'm afraid those days are long gone. You've been reading too many Miss Marple stories.'

Reg sighed. 'That's a shame. In fact, the police officers were painfully correct, left me alone in this little empty room for hours, and then a couple came in and started asking polite questions.' He gave a cautious laugh. 'They were at great pains to tell me I was there voluntarily, to help their enquiries, but I kept waiting for the trouble to start. You know, for real, like in the news when they break up demonstrations. I thought they'd punch me in the head. Instead, they wrote down everything I said, took it away, typed it up and got me to sign it.'

'Did you read it first?' Max asked.

'Every word.' Reg was starting to look more like himself. 'Not a thing I could complain about except for a few fancy British phrases.'

'Did they offer you a solicitor?'

He shook his head.

'But you weren't under caution?'

Reg shook his head. 'Not so far as I know. I'm not even sure what that means on this side of the pond.'

Max said, 'They would have told you. In fact, you could have walked out of there any time you wanted to.'

'No kidding?'

Bear, seeing nothing dramatic was about to happen, climbed awkwardly onto the sofa next to Reg, hung his head over the arm and fell asleep.

Libby watched Reg, wondering. Had he truly been so thrown by his experience in the police station? He hadn't been hand-cuffed or manhandled. Why was he so worried? Was it really because he was black or was there some other reason for his anxious state?

'Reg,' she said. 'I think you ought to come clean. Was it you who gave Mandy a note, inviting her to meet you? It seems to me the police wouldn't pull you in for no reason, so what's going on that scared you so? It can't just be spending time with PC Ian Smith, even though he's a bit of a thug.'

Reg sat back, running a finger round the top of his glass until it gave out a high-pitched whine. Both canine heads lifted. 'Can't fool you, Libby, can I? The truth is, it wasn't the time with your very polite and deferential police that rattled me. It was the attack on Mandy.' As Max refilled Reg's glass, the American said, 'I ought to explain. You see, I've been on a case in England, tracking down the theft of antiques – including my specialism, rare books. Valuable books have gone missing, sold on the auction market, bought by money launderers who then sell them on – the same old story.'

'I must say,' Libby put in, 'and this may not be relevant, but I wouldn't choose you for undercover work. You're far too noticeable.'

'It's all strictly above board. No disguises. I'm just following the trail of a few missing old books. You'll be pleased to know that Wells Cathedral and your librarian friend Dr Phillips are not involved. I just seized the chance to come to Somerset.' He swirled liquid around in his glass, gazing into its depths. 'I wanted to see young Mandy again.'

Libby drew a sharp breath.

Reg looked up. 'I know, you think I treated her badly. Maybe I did. Took advantage of her. But she's a special young woman, and the truth is, I could feel myself getting drawn in. I could imagine settling down with her, making a life together.' He rolled his eyes. 'I must have been crazy, but I told her, back then, when we were together, that I wanted a future with her. I would have married her, you know.'

'Really? She never said.'

His sad smile tore at her heart. 'That's Mandy. She knows how to keep a secret. She thought about it for a while, and then she said no.' He drained his glass. 'That was quite the shock to my ego, I can tell you. I thought I was offering her a great life that would bowl her over, but she decided she'd rather stay with Steve. She said it was a difficult decision, she liked me as a friend, but we were too different. You know, the usual blah- blah.' He shook his head. 'Thing is, it had always been me saying that stuff. I don't know what that young man had, apart from his musical talent, but I didn't stand a chance against him.'

Max said, 'They're planning to move in together, now.'

'I guess Mandy knew what she was doing, back then,' Reg said. 'I'd fallen for her quirkiness; that Goth thing she has going? Seeing her at the abbey that night, with Steve, I could tell she'd made the right choice. They have something special. I've moved on, but I still have one giant-sized soft spot for her and if I ever get my hands on her attacker, they're going to be sorry they picked on her.'

Libby fell silent, thinking once more of her young friend, helpless in hospital. 'Me too,' she muttered.

Max said, 'So what happened with Crystal?'

Reg winced. 'I guess I'm just not made for marriage, unlike you guys.'

'Maybe you haven't met the right person, yet,' Libby suggested.

His grin was sheepish. 'I don't know about that, but Somerset seems to be a good place for me to look.'

Libby and Max shared a glance. Libby's antennae were sending frantic signals, and judging by the light in his eyes, Max had picked up the tone of Reg's voice.

Max refilled his glass. 'Are you saying you've met someone else? You've only been here for five minutes.'

Reg laughed. 'Can't fool you, Max. And I can't hang around, at my age.'

'Well, who is she?' Libby demanded. 'Come on, don't keep us in suspense.'

He shook his head. 'No, it hasn't got that far, yet. I'll let you know if the time comes.' He clapped his hands together. 'Now, that's enough about my unsuccessful love life. What were we talking about?'

'Money-laundering through rare books. Any particular kind?' Max enquired.

'There's quite a market in Victorian works at the moment. You know, books making sense of past history for the nineteenth-century sensibility. We've found a few in other cathedral libraries, in fact. Hereford, for one.'

Libby raised her eyebrows. 'You mean, books that rewrite history to make it fit? That sounds like a familiar idea. So far as I can tell, all history books make the past fit the present. Almost everything I learned at school seems to be wrong, or at least, biased.'

Reg said, 'Anyway, after what happened at the abbey, I've been doing a little research of my own into these old Victorian tomes and I found something that will interest you two.' He bent down, opened his briefcase and pulled out a pile of photocopies. 'It's a long time since I did any serious research, but I found a couple of interesting things. The Victorians were keen to revive the old Gothic trends, especially the architecture of old churches and, of course, monasteries, so I looked up Cleeve Abbey and found a few details. As you know, your Henry VIII was in huge amounts of debt and the churches and monasteries were, often, very wealthy.'

Libby put in, 'But not our abbey at Cleeve. According to the guidebooks, it was quite badly off, existing on about £150 a year and giving a quarter of that to the poor.'

'Which is why,' Reg gave her an appreciative nod, 'it was sold off early, along with other small monasteries. The richer ones survived a few years longer, when Henry still couldn't balance his books. Part of Cleeve Abbey became a farmhouse, but there seems to have been confusion over who bought some of the land. Much of it went eventually to the owners of Dunster Castle, nearby, but there were some parcels of land bought by other landowners.' He put the book on the table. 'Look, three other purchasers. Master Inns, Master Moir, and,' he paused, dramatically, 'Master Wendlebury.'

Max grinned triumphantly at Reg. 'This Wendlebury who bought some of the abbey land must be an ancestor of our Chesterton Wendlebury. It's not exactly a common name, like Smith.'

Libby said, 'And the house Chesterton's currently living in, which belongs to this cousin of his, is called Priory Manor. It must have been built on that parcel of abbey land.'

Max shrugged. 'Possibly. And look,' he pointed to the figures written in spindly writing. 'If my understanding of the currency of the time is right, the sixteenth-century Wendlebury seems to have bought it for a song – £22 5s 6d. That sounds cheap, even for those days, which leads me to wonder whether that was the total price paid, or whether money changed hands under the table.'

Libby sat back. 'I'd no idea the Wendleburys had owned the place for hundreds of years.'

Max said, 'Unfortunately, it doesn't take us any farther in our quest to find out who attacked Mandy, does it?'

'I suppose not,' Libby sighed and turned to their visitor. 'Reg, why are you smiling to yourself?'

His face split into the widest grin she'd seen for a long time.

'Because you're not the only ones around here showing an interest in these old books. I had an email from Tom Reeves, that grumpy guy from the abbey, asking me about old books that mention Cleeve Abbey. I'd mentioned my interest to him at the abbey that night. I think he has some kind of axe to grind about the land. Something about planning permission for houses and spoiling the countryside?'

Libby laughed. 'Well, you're welcome to Tom Reeves, miserable old curmudgeon that he is. He got really mad when Jemima discovered the bones.' She broke off in mid-sentence. 'Oh. I wonder...'

Max's eyes met hers. 'I wonder too. Should we be looking more closely at Tom Reeves? As Reg says, he was in the abbey that night and, apparently, carrying out his own research.'

'But what possible motive could he have for attacking Mandy?'

Max sighed. 'Absolutely none, so far as I can see. I don't expect he'd even met her before the day of the picnic.'

Well,' Reg said. 'I'll leave you two alone to read these records and get back to my place in Bristol.'

'Why not stay here?' Libby offered.

Reg grinned. 'No, I like to drive at night.'

Max and Libby exchanged a glance. Reg seemed keen to get back. Was that anything to do with his hints about a new relationship?

It was late by the time Rex left, cheered by the curry Libby shared between the three of them.

'You make even a frozen curry taste like manna from heaven,' he said, as he gave her one of his giant hugs.

She smothered a yawn as she closed the door. Max was still in his study, immersed in the documents Reg had left. 'Are you coming to bed?'

He waved a hand. 'Not yet. This is too fascinating. There's a lot more detail about the sale of the abbey land. But you go, I'll be up later.'

'Not likely. If you've found something, I want to know about it. Coffee, that's what I need. Just give me a minute.'

When she returned, Max showed her several pages from the old book. 'Look,' he said. 'You remember the monk – our monk, we think – made that note about a theft in the book he was working on?'

'Yes. I thought someone might have stolen a crucifix or something.'

'Well, according to this book – Victorian, remember, so it could be all hearsay – it wasn't any object that was stolen. It was some of the land. The book mentions a dispute that went to the Court of Augmentations.'

Libby giggled. 'The what?'

Max took her coffee cup out of her hands. 'You've had enough of that. It's making you hysterical.'

'But, honestly, was there really such a thing?'

'Absolutely. Henry set it up to make sure he squeezed every penny from the sale of monastic land. The court made the final decisions. But this writer talks about bribery and says that local farmers and smallholders lost their businesses supplying food and so on to the monks, and they were pushed off their own land.'

'OK, so are you suggesting Wendlebury's ancestors did a deal with this Court of Augmentations to get their land?'

'That's exactly it. And, by the way, the man at the top of the

Court of Augmentations was one of Henry VIII's appointees, called Sir Richard Rich.'

'You're kidding. What a name. Perfect.' Her laughter died away. 'But do you really think some ancient grudge has anything to do with the attack on Mandy, or the death of our monk?' She thought about it. 'Maybe Bernard knew what was going on, because he made his cryptic note about a theft. What if someone had him killed because of that?'

Max was beaming with delight. 'In which case, we've solved the mystery of the murdered monk.'

'Not exactly. We're jumping to all sorts of conclusions, and we still don't know who killed him – we just have a possible reason why.'

'Well, even that deserves a lie-in tomorrow,' he said.

Libby yawned again, and tugged Max's arm. 'So, time for some kip. You've done a great job. Tomorrow, you can solve the mystery of Jack the Ripper's identity, but for now, come to bed.'

As they walked upstairs, she asked, 'Are we taking Reg off our suspect list? He seemed to be genuinely worried about Mandy.'

Max said, 'I don't think he'd have come around here if he'd attacked her. He was really upset and he'd had a bad day. I'm willing to give him the benefit of the doubt.'

Libby frowned. 'Maybe. Although, I don't like the way he goes through women. How many wives was it? You don't think he came to England hoping to whisk Mandy off her feet?'

'Possibly. Which would rule him out still further from attacking her.'

'Unless she rejected him. He normally seems so calm – the epitome of cool – but he was properly rattled when he first arrived, tonight. Maybe we keep him on the list, but not at the top.'

'So, who's at the top of your list?' Max asked.

Libby swirled coffee in her mug. 'Wendlebury, definitely. "Call me Ches," indeed. Repulsive man. And then, there's—'

'Tom Reeves.' Max was nodding. 'There's bad blood between him and Wendlebury, and he's furious about this planned housing development of the Wendleburys. I wonder if it's true that they'll close up some of the right-to-ramble spaces he's so fond of.'

'I read in the local paper there's a real battle going on about those houses. Half the parish wants them, the other doesn't, and there's the Exmoor Society who have a say. It's one of those local planning issues that sets neighbours against each other. I bet half the district aren't talking to the other half.' Libby groaned. 'So much to unpick, and none of it seems to relate to Mandy. The only thing our suspects have in common is their presence at the ghost hunt.'

33

'We need to tackle Tom Reeves,' Max said, the next day.

Libby agreed. 'He's been an outsider from the beginning of the whole Cleeve Abbey business. He wasn't part of the society picnic, he just turned up when the bones were found.'

'And he's been on the perimeter ever since – coming to one of your Exham History Society meetings and to the ghost hunt, but putting everyone's backs up with his bad temper.'

Libby was nodding. 'And his poor wife goes everywhere with him, looking as though she'd rather be someplace else. They're a strange pair. I'd love to know more about them.'

'Me too. But how best to approach them?'

They were sitting in the garden, under a massive parasol, a table by their side bearing jugs of iced water. The June sun beat down. A gentle breeze stirred the air. Bear lay close behind in the shade cast by a stunning bush covered in white flowers. Neither Libby nor Max could remember what it was called, but it flowered every year. Shipley, full of energy as always, was nosing around the foxgloves and geraniums at the bottom of the garden, returning to the pond at intervals to watch young newts popping up between the lily leaves.

Libby said, 'I feel too lazy to move, in this weather. I'm glad I don't go into the café so often. Although I'll be busy baking in a day or two. I've come up with some new recipes and I need to try them out.'

Max turned to look at her. 'That gives me an idea,' he said.

She groaned. 'That sounds ominous. Is it an idea that means we have to move?'

Max stood up. 'Afraid so. You know the café's the best place for information.'

'Ye-es.' Libby sipped at her water.

'Angela will be there, today, won't she?'

Libby let out a deep sigh. 'Are you suggesting I go into the café today, to talk to her about the Reeves?'

Max grabbed Libby's hand and pulled her to her feet. 'Well, she knows so many people, and she hears things, working in the café every day. Come on. I'll come too and buy you an ice cream. And we can tell Angela about our idea for Bear to visit Mandy.'

Libby peeped in through the window of the Crusts and Crumbs Café. Inside, Angela was in her element. The café was packed, and the extra waitresses she'd hired and trained worked like a well-oiled machine, providing tea, cakes made to Libby's recipes, and ice creams, to the overheated Exham visitors who'd retired, pink-faced and happy, from the heat of the beach.

Angela looked up as Libby and Max arrived and smiled serenely. 'Hello. I wasn't expecting you, today.'

Libby shook her head. 'I know, I was in the garden in my

shorts when Max had his bright idea. He thinks you might be able to help. But first, any news on Mandy?'

'Baby steps, I'm afraid,' Angela said. 'But there's a little improvement. The doctors and therapists are pleased, but Mandy's getting so frustrated. It's painful to watch.'

Libby explained their idea of taking Bear into the hospital. 'There's a great deal of paperwork to do first, of course; it's the NHS, after all, but Max already has a handle on that because of Shipley's sessions with Dr Sheffield.'

Angela's face broke into a delighted grin. 'Such a good idea. She's utterly fed up. Steve's there almost the whole time, playing that dreadful music she loves so much. You know, she can sing all the words to the songs, but she can't say anything she wants to. Isn't that odd?'

Max nodded. 'A strange thing, the human brain.'

Angela put down the plate of scones she was holding. 'Now, come into the kitchen, Libby, and tell me why else you've come. I can see you're on someone's trail.'

'I'll take the dogs on the beach for a few minutes,' Max said. 'We won't be long as it's so hot, but they can cool off in the sea.'

Libby followed Angela into the relative quiet of the kitchen. 'You're right. We're wondering about Tom Reeves and his wife, and we wondered if you knew anything about them.'

Angela said, 'I've known Winifred for years, and I feel so sorry for her.'

'She didn't grow up in Exham, though, or Max would have known her.'

'No, I met her when I volunteered at Wells Cathedral, a few years ago. She's a kind soul. She still helps out there. I think being in the cathedral helps her.'

Libby picked up a tiny iced cake and nibbled at the candied violet on the top. 'I imagine Tom isn't a religious man?'

'He was, at one time. He was a church warden, one of the lay helpers in the cathedral, until the tragedy.'

'Tragedy? I hadn't heard. What happened?'

Angela pushed crumbs of Victoria sponge cake around her plate. 'It was their son, Freddy. He went away to work in London, sharing a flat with his cousin. They got in with a bad crowd, and he died.'

'Drugs?'

Angela nodded and a shiver went up Libby's spine. Thank heaven her own children had escaped that curse. 'Every mother's worst fear. Did he overdose?'

'No. Winifred and Tom took a trip to London to visit him one day, out of the blue, thinking they'd surprise him. They took a casserole and an apple pie. They found him in his room, high, barely able to talk. As you can imagine, Tom let rip. He told Freddy exactly what he thought of him. It was quite a scene, Winifred told me. She was horrified. Freddy threw the apple pie at the wall and shouted at them to get out. Which they did. But, a few weeks later, the police were in touch. Freddy had been run over by a taxi. Apparently, he'd run out into the road, straight in front of it. There was nothing the driver could do to avoid him.'

'Still high, I suppose?'

Angela grimaced. 'That's the most tragic part. Apparently, he'd been trying to get clean. He'd stopped taking the drugs – but without professional help. He had some kind of detox crisis, hallucinations and so on. No one knows what he was running from when he ran into the road. There were no drugs in his system. He'd stopped taking them right after Tom and Winifred visited.'

Libby let out a low whistle. 'No wonder Tom never got over it. What a dreadful thing to happen, just when his son was trying to get clean.'

Angela sighed. 'Tom blamed everyone – Freddy's friends, Freddy himself for leaving Somerset, and I think sometimes Tom even blamed Winifred. But mostly, of course, he blames himself.'

The two women sat in silence for a moment, wondering what life must be like for Tom and Winifred, now their only son had gone.

Libby spoke first. 'I'm glad you told me about it. I can almost forgive Tom for the chip on his shoulder.'

'Exactly. Winifred says he dwells on things – the time when Freddy was at home, happy on the farm and loving the countryside, and Tom seems to be on a crusade to keep the land exactly as it was when Freddy was young. He opposes any changes – and especially, any new houses for incomers, like the housing estate the Wendleburys are planning. And Winifred, of course, is caught up in all this.' Angela straightened her already neat blouse and smiled. 'Anyway, I must get back to work. I was glad when the Reeves joined the History Society. I thought it might help them to be part of a group of people who also love Somerset. Jemima, and the Halfsteads, not to mention Archie Phillips and Quentin Dobson; the society members are really quite special, aren't they?'

Just then, Max returned, two wet, happy dogs at his side, to buy Libby the promised ice cream.

'You know,' she said as they walked home through the maze of quiet, leafy alleyways the summer visitors never saw, 'Angela's right about the Society. Members come and go, and there have been a few unfortunate events...'

Max interrupted. 'That's one way of putting it. Murders, you mean.'

Libby ignored him. 'The society's a kind of bedrock of knowledge. Especially since Jemima and her two acolytes joined. Maybe they can help Tom to relax a little and forgive himself. Always assuming he's not the killer,' she added.

Max kissed the top of her head. 'There's something healing about this part of the world. It took me a long time to learn to live with my daughter's death, and without Somerset, Exham and you, I wonder if I ever would. But I'll never get used to all those scary ladies in the society.'

'I don't know whether his story makes Tom more or less likely to have anything to do with the attack on Mandy,' Libby said, following her own thoughts. 'I'm worried about his temper. Could Mandy have done anything to anger him? I know she and Steve have dabbled in cannabis in the past, but I don't think they've taken anything stronger and I'm sure neither of them has been involved in... well, in selling drugs. But if they had, that might be a motive.'

Max took her hand. 'It's unlikely, given how well you know Mandy. The two of you were sharing the cottage until six months ago. I can't imagine either Mandy or Steve would have anything to do with drug dealing. But it's still a remote possibility.'

'I'll talk to our friend, DC Gemma,' Libby said. 'Maybe the police will know where drug supplies in the area come from.'

Libby spent the next day in the Crusts and Crumbs Café, working quietly in the kitchen at the back, baking. 'It's just not the same without Mandy,' she confessed to Angela. 'Has she remembered anything about the attack?'

Angela shook her head. 'DC Gemma came in and showed her pictures of everyone at the abbey, but she couldn't say who attacked her. Maybe she didn't even see them at the time – it was dark and she seems to have been attacked from behind. And she couldn't remember who sent her the note. I don't think she remembers much about it at all.'

Libby grabbed a handful of dough and slammed it on the work surface.

'You could use the machine to knead, you know,' Angela pointed out.

Libby grunted. 'I need to beat something up. I've found it helps.'

'Good idea. I'll join you.'

The two women pummelled bread dough while Annabel scurried around the café, serving summer visitors. Finally, having beaten the bread into submission, they dropped portions into baskets to rise and went back through the door to the serving area.

Gladys, Libby's friend from the flower shop, was seated at one of the tables. She raised an arm in salute to Libby, immediately returning to her animated conversation with her companion, a well-built man wearing a shiny suit just a little too tight for his size.

Angela muttered, 'Gladys' latest conquest. He runs a souvenir shop in Minehead, near to the village where Gladys told me she's buying a new house. He makes a fortune, I've heard. He has his fingers in all sorts of local pies.'

'Does he?' Libby looked up. 'What sort of things?'

Angela shrugged. 'Local politics, I believe. He's on the planning committee of the local council.'

'Is he indeed?' Libby thought for a moment. 'How long has he been seeing Gladys?'

Angela pushed a stray hair behind one ear. 'Not long. Her last one went back to Wales at the weekend. I'm not sure where she met this chap.' She smiled. 'You can ask her. He's just leaving and you know what Gladys is like. She can't keep anything to herself for two minutes.'

Sure enough, as Angela left to answer a query from Annabel, Gladys came over to Libby. Her cheeks were flushed with pleasure. Gladys was a most attractive woman, and the proprietor of a thriving business, recently enlarged and revamped as the result of a legacy. She might be an easy target for men with more interest in her bank balance than herself. But it was none of Libby's business. Gladys was an intelligent grown-up.

'What do you think, now, Libby?' she asked, turning to watch her companion walk away down the High Street. 'Is he after my money, or what?'

Libby laughed out loud, relieved. She should have known Gladys could look after herself.

'What about this dreadful business with Mandy, though?' Gladys said. 'Terrible state of affairs. Just terrible. Who could do such a thing?'

'We just don't know.' Libby described Mandy's current condition.

Gladys shook her head. 'She's such a cheerful young thing,' she said. 'Let's hope she remembers what happened soon.'

Libby changed the subject. Talking about Mandy tied her stomach in knots. 'I heard on the grapevine that you're thinking of buying a new house in West Somerset.'

'That's right.' Gladys said. 'I came into some money when my sister died. I have my eye on renovating a little thatched cottage just outside Minehead.' That reminded Libby of Rosalind's cottage. 'Pretty little place,' Gladys continued. 'Right in the countryside. For weekends, you know. So much nicer than spending all my time living over the shop. But it's complicated.'

'Why's that?' Libby was only listening with half an ear. Gladys was like a wind-up clock. You gave her a subject, set her off, and she would talk for hours.

'Oh, the planning,' Gladys threw her hands in the air. 'You wouldn't believe the hoops I'm having to jump through. Not that I mind too much – the planning officer's rather a lovely young man,' she chuckled.

Libby raised her eyebrows.

Gladys had the grace to blush. 'The windows and doors have to be just so, in keeping with the age of the property – it's a couple of hundred years old – and the planning committee at the council want to know every tiny detail. It's coming up at the next parish council meeting, you know. I shall be going and not just because of my little place. There's going to be such a to-do.' Her eyes were bright with excitement.

Libby said, 'What sort of to-do?'

'There are objections to plans for another building. Chesterton Wendlebury, over at Priory Manor, wants to build a housing estate. Well, it's his cousin's place, the politician, but Chesterton's handling everything. Strange man, is Chesterton. Good-looking in his way – but his reputation's terrible. I'm staying clear of him.' She broke off. 'Now, where was I?'

'A planning application?'

'That's right. There's been a parish poll about it.'

Her attention caught, Libby said, 'What's a parish poll?'

'Well,' Gladys leaned comfortably over the counter, 'anyone can call a parish poll if they get enough signatures, to ask if local people want a new development. Of course, whoever sets it up has to pay for the poll, and the results aren't binding, so I can't see the point.' She nodded, sagely. 'They had a poll about the plans. Only about a hundred people voted out of three thousand, and fifty per cent voted against. So, the council is no farther forward. They're going to sort it all out at the meeting and I can't wait. It will be lively, you can be sure.' Gladys rubbed her hands together. 'You should come along. It's an open meeting and it will cheer you up no end. I often go, just for the entertainment. Why don't you come with me to hear my plans approved?'

Libby grinned. 'Wild horses wouldn't keep me away.'

* * *

Later that day, Libby called DC Gemma. 'Is it a good time?' she asked as the police officer answered her phone.

'Libby. I'm always pleased to talk to you,' Gemma said, so charmingly that Libby almost believed her. 'I'm in Exham at the moment, doing some home visits – nothing exciting – but I'm just about to come off duty. Shall I pop over? You can feed me cake. Give me fifteen minutes to change?'

Libby just had time to make up a jug of something cold. Once settled in the garden under the parasol, Gemma kicked off her shoes and stretched bare legs to the sun. 'Glorious day, isn't it?'

'Try this,' Libby said, offering her a glass containing various pieces of fruit.

'Can't drink – I have to drive home and I'm terrified of being pulled up for drink-driving – that would be the end of my career.'

'It's a mocktail,' Libby pointed out. 'All the taste but none of the alcohol.' As Gemma sipped, she went on, 'I gather you may be in line for promotion.'

Gemma almost choked on the drink. 'How did you know?'

Libby burst out laughing. 'Lucky guess. Well, Max's guess, actually, helped by Joe. Acting Detective Sergeant, is it?'

Gemma blushed brick-red. 'That's right. And Ian Smith's furious.'

'Well Ian Smith's a prat. Congratulations. It's well deserved.'

'Thank you.'

They talked of Mandy for a while. Gemma, just a few years older than Mandy, shivered.

'My mother's convinced something like that will happen to me. She was pleased when I moved into CID, though. She thought it would be safer than being a bobby on the beat, but she's changed her mind. She says Somerset's turning into the murder capital of the country. Mandy's attack would have been the final straw, if it weren't for the promotion. Now my mother thinks I can sit in an office and send the constables to do the dangerous stuff.'

'Parents never really know what their children are doing. I

think it's best to let them get on with it. But the reason I was keen to talk to you was about drugs.'

Gemma let out a shout of laughter. 'If you want advice on how to get your hands on them, you're looking in the wrong place.'

'I am, but not in the way you think.' Libby described her conversation with Angela. 'And it led us – Max and me – to wonder whether either Mandy or Steve had been involved with drugs.'

Gemma shook her head, frowning. 'Mandy? Seriously?'

Libby threw her hands in the air. 'I'm clutching at straws, really. There seems to be no motive for the attack.'

Gemma, in Acting DS mode, was thoughtful. 'I'd say a definite no, except that you can never really be sure. I know of a few likely users and dealers, even though they've never been charged. There's often not enough evidence. I've never seen either Mandy's or Steve's name come up at work, though. I'll ask around, just in case, but I think it's a long shot.'

Libby sighed. 'That's good news. I'm sure it's a red herring – Mandy's very law-abiding, despite the Goth cloaks and face rings. Even her tattoos are mostly fake. I just want to get to the bottom of things. If there's no motive for anyone to hurt Mandy, then why did it happen? What on earth was going on?' She stopped talking.

'What is it?' Gemma said.

Libby shook her head. 'Sorry. For a second, I had one of those half-thoughts that pops into your head and then disappears. You know, an idea that goes away before you can catch it. Like a dream you can't remember.'

'Try to think,' Gemma urged. 'Was it something I said? Something about drugs?'

'No, I don't think so.' Libby heaved a heavy sigh. 'Not to worry. It will come back to me. I don't expect it was important.' Her phone rang and she excused herself to answer. 'Rosalind?'

'Now, Mrs Forest,' she purred, at her most persuasive. 'I wanted to ask a little favour.'

'Yes?' Libby was non-committal.

'You see, I'd like to go back to the abbey. We had to end our ghost hunt early, of course, but we did think we'd seen something in the refectory. Now, I'm not suggesting we spend another night there...'

Just as well. Libby would never spend another night in a haunted place so long as she lived.

Rosalind seemed to take her silence for interest. 'Good, I plan to visit again during daylight, but I've heard about one of the dogs you brought when you visited – Shirley, is it?'

'Shipley.'

'Quite. I hear he has a wonderful nose.'

'He detects illnesses, not ghosts,' Libby retorted.

'But he might be able to sense things. From the past. Don't you think it's worth a try?'

Before Libby could object, Rosalind had rattled off a date and time, and rung off.

35

BEAR

Max and Libby walked the dogs early, next morning, while the air was cool and the grass dewy. 'Don't you love this time of day?' Libby said.

'I do once I'm up and dressed. It's the getting up that's hard. Especially these days, now my bones are starting to creak. You realise I'll be sixty in a year or so?'

Libby planted a kiss on his cheek. 'Poor old man. At least you still have all your hair.' She trailed her hands through the long, damp grass as they set off up the Knoll, Shipley running ahead, for there were no sheep on the hill today. Bear plodded at their sides. Suddenly, he stopped, sniffed the air and set off after Shipley.

'Bear's so much better since he's been taking his medication,' Libby said. 'I'm sure he has many more years in him.'

Max agreed. 'He was sniffing around the drawing room the other day, as though all our talk of ghosts and history reminded him of that time we thought there was a ghost in Exham House. But how would he know?'

'He understands a lot of what we say,' Libby said, 'especially if it's about food or walks, but I don't think his vocabulary's up to words like "haunting" or "spooky".

'You never know. We used all those "ghostly" words at that time. Maybe he remembers how they sounded.'

Libby stopped walking, and turned to look at Max, her hands on her hips. 'And you were always the biggest sceptic. Don't tell me you've started to believe all the paranormal stuff?'

Max shook his head. 'Don't forget, we saw something at the abbey that looked very much like a spirit wafting through the wall, just before we were all distracted by Steve finding Mandy. No one talked about it, afterwards. We were all too worried about her to care, but there was definitely something happening.'

'Did your new friend Charlie have anything to say about it?' Libby had started back up the hill, keeping her face hidden. She didn't want to admit, even to herself, that she was a touch jealous of Charlie, but the younger woman was so clever, so funny, and looked so attractive that anyone would feel a tiny stab of envy. She'd rung Max once or twice, telling him about delays in using the AMS to investigate their monk, because of exams at the university. 'I'm afraid we have to put the students first,' she'd said. Each time she rang, Libby had pretended not to mind.

Max was laughing. 'My new friend? Libby, I do believe you're jealous.'

'Nonsense. Of course I'm not. Well, not very. But the two of you do get along very well.'

Max took her arm. 'I'm flattered that you're jealous,' he said, 'at my time of life, because Charlie can't be much older than thirty-five despite all her qualifications. That's the same age as Joe. Of course I like and admire her, but you're the one I love. You're just as clever as she is, in a different way.'

Libby threw a handful of grass at him. 'In a different way?'

'I rather spoiled that compliment, didn't I? And I was doing so well. Sorry.' He grinned, not looking at all sorry. 'Anyway, to answer your question, Charlie didn't have much time for what she called "an apparition probably caused by light shining on dust, if not by our overheated imaginations". She belongs to the school of science that says everything has to be proven and if you can't replicate an experiment there's no proof.'

'Well, that makes perfect sense. But there have been several sightings and maybe we'll see another if we visit again. Even Cleeva Clapp thought there was something in it.'

'But she was selling admission to the abbey when she wrote that in her pamphlet,' Max objected.

Libby remembered, 'Rosalind asked us to take Bear and Shipley with us when we go to the abbey. I'm sure they'll be able to tell if there's anything strange there.'

Max stopped walking. 'That's a great idea. They'd love it.'

'But it will be odd, being there again.'

Max shot a look at her. 'You're thinking about Mandy. But it wasn't a ghost that slipped a note to her that night, or tried to kill her.'

Libby nodded. 'And going back might clarify things. You know, we can retrace our steps that night, see if anything jogs our memories. I still feel a bit vague about what happened. There were so many people, all moving around, that it's difficult to get a grip on who has an alibi and who hasn't. If we think it through in situ, we might be able to get a firmer handle on things.'

They reached the top of the Knoll, and looked around. Somerset shimmered in the sun's haze.

Max said, 'Just look at it. No wonder we all love the place.' He swept an arm in a wide gesture, taking in many acres of fields. 'I think Tom translates some of his love for his son into his feelings about the countryside. He's so dogmatic about rights of way and land ownership, as though he's saving it on behalf of his son. And his son will never know.'

'Poor man,' Libby said. 'If only he could lose all that anger.'

'Well, he'll no doubt be at the council meeting, so brace yourself,' Max said.

36

COUNCIL MEETING

Libby's daily check-in with Angela the next day revealed no real change in Mandy's condition, although she was gaining strength. Max, seeing Libby's drawn face, wished he could think of a way to cheer her up. At least his son Joe and wife Claire were coming tomorrow for dinner. Maybe Robert and Sarah would like to join them. That would cheer Libby like nothing else. They could spend the evening in baby talk.

Libby's eyes lit up at the suggestion of a proper family party. 'You're a genius,' she said. 'And maybe Ali could come as well?'

Max turned away so Libby couldn't see as he made a face, screwing his eyes up and tensing his shoulders. He'd never forgiven Ali for jetting off to Brazil to save the world before she finished her degree, leaving Libby distraught.

Libby said, 'I can see what you're doing. You're making that face. I can tell from behind, you know, and you need to get over this thing with Ali. She came to our wedding, don't forget.'

'Hm. Very noble of her.'

'Besides, she was so upset when she had that miscarriage. Cut her some slack, Max.'

'OK,' he held his hands up. 'I give in. I will phone her myself and invite her to come to dinner tomorrow and bring that boyfriend of hers if he's currently gracing England with his presence. I think you said he would be here for a few days? And, in return, can I invite Reg? He's begging for more of your cooking.'

Libby breathed a deep sigh. 'Of course. Oh, and tell him to bring a plus-one. If he's already picked up a nice English girl, I want to meet her.'

* * *

Libby met Gladys outside the offices of the district council that evening.

'The parish council meet in the Council Chambers,' Gladys told her. 'It's very grand. Oh, look,' she pointed to a corpulent, smiling man entering the building. 'That's Alf Higgins. He's one of the councillors on the planning committee – and several of the other committees as well.'

'So, he has his fingers in all the pies. No wonder he's so enormous.'

Arranging their faces into suitably sober expressions, they headed inside and took their seats towards the back of the chamber,. Tom Reeves, two rows ahead, glanced back at them and looked away.

A hush fell over the room as the chair, a tall, imposing lady wearing two sets of glasses, one sitting on her nose, the other hanging on a chain around her neck, called the meeting to order.

Gladys' application for planning consent was agreed quickly, with only one half-hearted objection, and Gladys let out a cheer.

Madam Chair glared.

Libby heard movement to one side and turned to look,

meeting the eyes of a vaguely familiar journalist. She turned away as the meeting continued on to the next item on the agenda.

'Plans submitted by Mr Laurence Wendlebury to build 55 homes on Priory Manor land beside Abbey Mill. Mr Wendlebury will be represented by his cousin, Mr Chesterton Wendlebury.' Madam Chair looked around, 'Is Mr Wendlebury here?'

As she spoke, a commotion interrupted, causing heads to turn as Chesterton Wendlebury arrived amid a flurry of apologies.

Sighing, two members of the public shifted along to allow him to sit in the front row of observers. Madam Chair eyed him with frown and asked the planning officer to report.

The application was fiercely contested.

'Local people are worried about incomers trespassing on their land.'

'Rich and powerful landowners can't stop progress.'

'Homeowners have rights.'

'Farmers' land's being ruined,' someone shouted.

'Incomers want their way.' A portly councillor, red in the face, rose from his seat. 'Don't care what damage they do.'

'No second homes in Somerset,' someone shouted.

Madam Chair banged on the desk, but by now the councillors were shouting over one another.

A single voice rose above the hubbub, bellowing, 'Just what we'd expect from the Wendleburys.'

'I say.' Chesterton Wendlebury was on his feet. 'No need for that sort of talk—'

Tom Reeves leapt up from his seat and stepped into the aisle between the seats. 'We'll say what we like.' He was purple with fury. He lunged forward until he was only inches away from Wendlebury. His head just reached the taller man's chest. 'You're naught but a thief,' he shouted, poking his finger into Chesterton's stomach.

Wendlebury grabbed Reeves' shirt front. 'You little—' He lifted the man almost off his feet.

Reeves wriggled, gasping, from his grip and landed a left hook on his jaw.

Madam Chair hammered on the desk. 'That's enough,' she shouted.

The clerk grabbed Tom Reeves. Two burly councillors clutched Wendlebury's arms from behind.

Madam Chair pointed to the door. 'Out,' she shouted. 'Get out of my chamber.'

The reporter from the local paper followed Wendlebury and Reeves outside, phone held aloft, ready to capture every moment.

Gladys followed them out, Libby tagging along.

Wendlebury stumped towards his car, muttering into his yellow waistcoat and rubbing his cheek, with Tom Reeves still shouting at his departing back.

The reporter turned to Libby. 'Mrs Forest, I knew something would happen when I saw you arrive. There's always trouble around you. Any comment? I believe you were involved in Mr Wendlebury being sent to prison.'

Libby shook her head. 'Sorry. I've nothing to say.'

'Come on, now. There's something going on, isn't there? Won't you give us a little quote? Help to solve the mystery attack on the young woman at the abbey?'

Libby opened her mouth to give the reporter a piece of her mind. Then, she saw Max and the dogs watching from the corner. 'Absolutely no comment,' she said and walked away, her head high. The reporter trotted behind for a few paces, before giving up.

'What are you laughing at?' Libby demanded as she reached Max.

'If you could only see your face,' he said. 'I thought you were going to hit that poor journalist. Whatever's been going on at the council meeting?'

Libby described the fight. 'Anyway, you can read all about it in next week's local paper.'

'But what made you so angry? You looked murderous.'

Libby sighed. 'That reporter. She wanted to know about Mandy. It was as though she was accusing me of something, and as though the attack on Mandy was nothing more than an exciting titbit for her newspaper.'

'I'd no idea council members would behave like that,' Libby confessed as she sat with Max in The Country House Hotel near the council offices. 'I always thought their meetings must be deadly dull.'

The room buzzed with chatter. Today was the longest day of the year and diners were excited, many planning to spend the night on Glastonbury Tor waiting for the sun to rise.

Max said, 'There's never a dull moment in Somerset, is there?' He looked up from the menu. 'Feelings run high. There are a few landowners like the Wendleburys, who've been here for ever and seem to own half the county, while some of the others resent them for it. Tom Reeves has a good point. Why should the Wendleburys make a fortune out of selling off their land and at the same time stop the locals walking along paths they've been using for years?'

'But local people need affordable housing, don't they?'

The waiter came for their order.

Libby said, 'I'll have the hot smoked trout, crushed potatoes, beetroot and walnuts.'

Max made a face. 'Sounds strange.'

'Trust me, it's a combination made in heaven.'

'In that case, I'll have the same.' He returned the menu and the waiter headed off with their order. 'When it comes to food, I'll defer to your judgement. And, in fact, you're probably right about the planning problem. There are two sides to every dispute.' He took a long drink. 'Good stuff, this low-alcohol cider. Who would have thought it?' He leaned across the table. 'Maybe you should stand for Exham Town Council. I think you'd do a good job.'

'What?' Libby gasped. 'You're joking. I don't want to get into any fights, thank you. I like our quiet life.'

Max spluttered on his mouthful of cider. 'Quiet? You're joking.'

'I'm going to take a back seat in future.'

'Well, I'll believe that when it happens,' Max said.

They fell silent as the food arrived. Libby swallowed a forkful of trout and beetroot. 'Delicious,' she pronounced.

Max raised his glass. 'I'll drink to that.'

Libby ate for a while in silence.

'What's the matter?' Max asked.

'I was just thinking about the council meeting. It was vicious, that fight, and Tom Reeves was still furious when he left. Why was he so mad?'

'You told me – it was about planning permission.'

She shook her head. 'I think it was more than that. Tom had people on his side. Several of the other councillors were making his case and I had a feeling the vote might have gone his way. It never got so far because the chair deferred the vote to the next meeting. But Tom was still angry.' She laid her knife and fork together, neatly, on her plate. 'Max, this doesn't feel right. We need to do something.'

'Visit Tom Reeves?'

'Maybe.' She pushed her plate away. 'My antennae tell me something's badly wrong. Let's go and see him.'

Max took a final bite. 'You're right about the trout,' he admitted. 'It's delicious. I just hope you're wrong about Tom Reeves. But maybe it wouldn't hurt to talk to him.' He followed her from the restaurant, muttering. 'So much for taking a back seat.'

* * *

Winifred, as mouse-like as Libby remembered from the night of the ghost hunt, smiled nervously at Libby and Max but showed them into the sitting room of the bungalow without asking why they'd come. Perhaps years of her husband's put-downs had taught her not to ask questions.

The bungalow was almost new, sited near their farm, with nondescript magnolia-painted walls and a row of China animals lined up on the mantelpiece above the electric fire. The fire was turned off, but still the room, with a low roof, seemed stiflingly hot.

Winifred switched off the soap on the television and offered cups of tea, before turning to Max. 'Or something stronger? I know men like whisky – I think we have a bottle?' She waved an arm vaguely at a dark brown cabinet in the corner.

Max said, 'No, tea would be lovely. I'm driving, Mrs Reeves.'

'Oh, please do call me Winifred,' she said, with an anxious frown. 'Maybe a bourbon biscuit with your tea?'

Libby hid a smile. Winifred was not about to offer her a whisky. Winifred belonged to an earlier era where women looked after men.

They sat nursing small china cups of brown tea.

Winifred said, 'I'm sorry Tom isn't here. He was a little agitated after the council meeting. He's gone for a walk with

Timmy, our dog. It calms him down.' Her forehead creased. 'He gets a little... upset sometimes.'

Libby said, 'That was why we came to see him. To check all was well. I was at the council meeting and we were worried.'

Winifred sighed. 'He misses the farm, now he's retired.' She stood up, moving restlessly around the room. 'I like this little house. It's easier to look after than that old farmhouse, but it breaks Tom's heart every time he sees it with its new owners.' She murmured, as though to herself, 'He always wanted our Freddy to take over the farm tenancy when he retired.' She raised her voice. 'But you don't want to know about that, do you? Freddy's gone.'

Libby nodded. 'We heard. I'm so sorry for your loss. It must be very hard.'

Winifred smiled. 'No secrets in Somerset, are there? We still miss our son.'

Libby felt Max stiffen. He pointed at a small side table, covered by an embroidered cloth, holding a silver-framed photograph. 'Is that Freddy in the photo?'

Winifred picked up the frame, smoothing her hand over the glass. 'That's right. It's an old school photo. He's seven, in this.'

Libby looked closely. 'There's a strong likeness to Tom, isn't there?'

'Yes, and they worshipped each other.' Winifred breathed on the glass, polished it with a small handkerchief, and replaced the photo carefully.

Max said, 'We were so sorry to hear what happened to Freddy.'

Winifred's sigh seemed to come from deep within her. 'We warned him about drugs, but, like all young men, he thought he knew best. If only...' she blinked rapidly and sat down, her back ramrod straight. 'Still, it's no good dwelling on it, is it? Freddy chose to take drugs. In any case, it wasn't the drugs that killed him – it was a really stupid traffic accident. He was just careless. We can't go around blaming other people.'

Libby recognised in Winifred an indomitable soul, quietly soldiering on through life, despite its hardships. Feeling she could be frank, she said, 'We wanted to make sure Tom doesn't do anything silly or – you know – dangerous.'

Winifred smiled. 'Silly, yes, but not dangerous. I love Tom to bits and he can be foolish. But, generally, once he's been angry and shouted, he gets it out of his system with a pint or two in the local and feels better.'

Max rose. 'In that case, we won't trouble you any more. Thank you very much for the tea. I hope you didn't mind us dropping in like this.'

'Not at all. I like company. Please come again at any time. And don't worry about Tom. I can handle him.' And, once more, Libby caught a glimpse of the backbone of steel under Winifred's mild-mannered surface.

They climbed into the car for the drive back towards Exham.

Libby said, 'You know, I still have a bad feeling.'

'What about?' Max asked.

'Tom Reeves.'

He started the engine. 'You heard Winifred. She seems pretty sure he won't do anything.'

'I'd like to make sure. Let's call in at his local. It's only just down the lane.'

A few minutes later, Libby and Max drew up in the car park of Tom's local pub.

The place was full.

They stood in the doorway, methodically reviewing every face.

'Can't see him,' Max said.

'Nor can I.'

The man behind the bar waved in their direction. 'What can I get you, my lovers?' he asked in a broad West Country accent.

'We're just looking for someone – Tom Reeves. He's not at home. Do you know him?'

The barman raised his eyebrows. 'One of my best customers. Not tonight, though. No sign of him.'

A man at a nearby table turned to look at Libby. 'You were at that council meeting, weren't you?'

Libby recognised him. He'd tried to step in between Tom and Wendlebury.

He grinned. 'I go every month – always a to-do there. Better than the television. And this evening was a doozy.' He chuckled. 'A proper fist fight.'

Libby said, 'Have you seen Tom since?'

'No, not since then. He set off home in his car like a wild thing, but I don't know where he went if he's not at home.'

Libby and Max exchanged glances. 'You don't think—' Libby stammered, suddenly anxious. 'Would he go after Wendlebury?'

'We'd better find out.'

They ran out of the pub and jumped in the car.

'Priory Manor,' Max said, accelerating so that the wheels squealed.

Libby's heart thudded as they sped through the narrow lanes. The sun had finally gone down, and the roads were dark and twisty. Libby hung on to her seat in silence.

They turned in at a pair of ostentatious faux-classical columns marking a drive that led between neat hedges to a country house. It had been embellished over the years in a mix of styles, from authentic Tudor beams to late Victorian gothic arches.

Leaping from the car, the dogs at their heels, they ran to the door, and stopped, shocked. The door had been smashed open and hung, limply, from broken hinges.

Max peered closely at the marks around the hinges. 'Shotgun pellets, by the look of it.' He pushed the door wide. 'Wendlebury. Are you in here?'

No one answered, but a bout of furious barking sounded from somewhere out of sight.

Libby held her breath as they moved into the spacious hall-way. 'Should we call someone?'

Suddenly, Max threw out his arm and stopped Libby in her tracks. 'Wait,' he said. 'There's something...'

At the foot of the stairs, Chesterton Wendlebury lay in a small pool of blood.

Max ran over, bent down, feeling for a pulse. He looked up at Libby, horrified, and shook his head. 'He's dead.'

'It looks as though Tom Reeves got to him, after all,' Max said.

The police had arrived, led by DCI Morrison, and shooed Max and Libby out of the house as they waited for the pathologist. Morrison listened to Libby and Max as they gave an account of the evening.

Libby shook her head. 'You heard what Winifred said – Tom's all talk.'

Max said, 'I'm afraid he's going to have a lot of explaining to do. At the moment, I'd put my money on him as the killer. I suppose Wendlebury pushed him too far over these houses. He's unbalanced – we've all seen him lose his rag over nothing.'

'He was raring for a fight at the council meeting. But let's not jump to conclusions,' Libby suggested.

Morrison said, 'Half the residents out in the countryside have shotguns. But there's no sign of the weapon and his death is more likely to be due to his falling down the stairs after the shooting.'

'So he was shot while he was upstairs?' Max asked.

Morrison nodded and went on. 'It looks as though someone

shot their way in as Wendlebury was on his way to bed. The sound of the break-in must have drawn him out of the bathroom – he'd taken off most of his clothes – and he was shot from the bottom of the stairs, according to the trajectory of the pellets.' He pointed to holes in the ceiling above the landing. 'Forensics will tell us if I'm right.' Morrison frowned. 'I'm telling you more than I should, of course. I can trust you to keep your mouths closed. But we'll need you to come to the station and give us proper statements as soon as possible.' He shook his head. 'Looks like an open-and-shut case, to me. But, as we know, things aren't always what they seem.'

Libby said, 'Any signs of burglary as the motive?'

Morrison guffawed. 'There's a man with a clear motive who's not where his wife says he should be at the time of the murder, and you look for someone else.'

Libby said, 'Yes, but just in case...'

'Since you ask, it seems the killer went upstairs after Wendlebury died. Stepped in the blood and smudged it – we might get a partial footprint out of that, with any luck. My men will get round to Reeves' place and collect his footwear. Mind you, these days, everyone wears the same boots or trainers. Still, it's something. Then, the killer went into the bedroom and ransacked the drawers. No idea what he took, though. There was a watch left there, and some silver cufflinks, not to mention laptops and other electricals, and some interesting china in some of the other rooms.'

Libby said, 'Poor old Chesterton Wendlebury. Just out of prison, and he's dead already. I don't know how I feel. Confused, I suppose, because I never liked him, but still, he didn't deserve this.'

Max said, 'You thought he was trying to kill you, once,'

'But he wasn't, as it turned out. He was just a bumbling fool without much of a moral compass. At the abbey, I thought he was a bit sad. He was so pleased to join us. I'm glad we were friendly to him.' She watched, biting back unexpected tears as Wendlebury's body, zipped securely inside a body bag, was loaded into an ambulance. 'And I'm going to make sure whoever killed him pays for it.'

Next day, Libby found Max already in the kitchen. He'd flung open the door to the garden, enjoying the prospect of another hot day. He turned as Libby arrived. 'Look at this. It's a perfect morning. I shall make breakfast for us both.'

'My head's spinning from last night. I woke up thinking of Chesterton Wendlebury. You know, I'm going to miss him, in a funny way.'

'Miss him like a sore head,' Max grunted. 'I couldn't stand the man.'

'No, but you must admit, he was a pretty memorable character with that yellow waistcoat and green cords. And when Tom Reeves attacked him at the council meeting, he was very restrained. He was much bigger than Tom, but he didn't make any attempt to hurt him.'

Max threw a ball for Bear to chase. 'Tom Reeves,' he muttered. 'Do you think he killed Wendlebury?'

Libby didn't answer at first. Slowly, she wandered down the garden, mulling over the events of yesterday, Max a pace or two behind. She bent and pulled up a handful of leaves from the border, hoping they were weeds. 'No,' she said at last. 'It doesn't add up. We know Tom was furious with Chesterton, but he was using the right channels, going through the council. I know he lost his temper at the meeting, but he's not the first person to resort to his fists. Local government drives people nuts, sometimes. He'd be crazy to start a fight with Chesterton and then shoot him, because, of course, he's the obvious culprit. Whatever else Tom may be, I don't think he's a fool.' She dropped the weeds in a nearby tub. 'In any case, the council haven't made their decision about the houses yet, and Tom seemed to have most of the councillors on his side. I won't be surprised if the planning application is refused. So, why would Tom kill Wendlebury, when he was already winning the argument?'

'That's why you suspected a burglary?'

'Exactly. I think the killer was looking for evidence of some sort.'

'Possibly something to prove the Wendleburys can't build on the land?'

Libby stopped in her tracks. 'Well, I was hoping for something different. Something that might take Tom out of the frame.' She sighed. 'Maybe you're right about him, after all.'

'Why don't you want Tom to be the killer?'

Libby rubbed at her face, leaving a smear of soil on her cheek, trying to decide exactly what she felt. 'Because I feel sorry for Winifred,' she said, at last. 'She lost her son. I can't bear to think she'll lose her husband as well. Besides, don't forget the attack on Mandy. I can't think of any reason at all why Tom Reeves would try to kill her.'

Max followed her back across the grass and into the kitchen. 'Something about information? Remember the note. What could Tom possibly know that might have made Mandy go into the gatehouse alone in the middle of the night?'

Libby held her head in her hands. 'It gets more complicated all the time. If only Mandy could tell us.'

Max turned on the cooker. 'And why would Mandy go on her own in response to a note, unless she knew what it was all about?'

Libby gasped. 'I should have realised before. We saw Mandy's face when Reg arrived. Seeing him again put her in a spin. I bet, when she read the note, she thought it was from him.'

Max stopped, holding an egg over a bowl, ready to crack it. 'But wouldn't she tell Steve?'

'Of course not,' Libby scoffed. 'Mandy was confused. The last thing she'd do would be to tell Steve. She'd need to hear what Reg had to say. So, she went to the gatehouse to find out what Reg wanted before risking her relationship with Steve.'

Max cracked the egg hard on the edge of a knife, missing the bowl. He watched the mess spread. 'It's true. Women are impossible to understand. And now look what's happened.'

Libby mopped up egg with sheets of kitchen paper and a damp J-cloth. 'Do you want me to finish making the breakfast?'

'No, I can manage. I was distracted for a moment; thinking. The note was typed.'

'So it was. Which means it was premeditated.'

'Which makes it even more confusing.' Max selected another egg. 'Maybe the would-be killer thought Mandy would recognise his writing. Who would she know that well?'

'Several people, including you and me. Then, there's Angela – and I really don't think we're including her as a suspect – Reg and Steve.' Libby thought for a moment. 'Oh dear, that makes Reg a suspect, again, but I really don't think it could be him. And there's no reason at all for him to shoot Chesterton Wendlebury.'

Max was concentrating on the stove. Libby tried hard not to watch what he was doing. It took all her self-control to avoid giving advice.

'Someone,' she murmured, 'must be linked both to our Tudor monk, to Mandy, and to the Wendlebury planning application. That's the only reason I can think of for the attack to happen in the abbey.' She shook her head. 'But there's absolutely no one that fits that description.'

Max's phone rang. 'Gemma,' Max whispered as he answered. 'Maybe this is our answer.' He raised his voice. 'DC Humberstone? How can I help you?' His face fell. 'Last night? Really? At the same time?'

'What is it?' Libby whispered.

Max shook his head as he spoke into the phone. 'We'll come straight over.' He ended the call and dropped his phone on the table. 'It seems there was even more excitement last night.'

'Why? What's happened?' Her stomach lurched. 'Not Mandy? She's been getting stronger every day even if she can't say much yet.'

'Don't panic. It's nothing like that, but while the police were out last night covering both the Wendlebury place and the summer solstice on Glastonbury Tor, someone broke into the museum at Watchet.'

'Quentin's museum? He wasn't hurt, was he?' Libby looked up, startled.

'He wasn't there – he was on Glastonbury Tor, Gemma says, watching the sunrise. It seems he's a Druid.'

'You're kidding. Quentin?' Libby thought about it. 'Actually, it makes sense. He's keen on history and spirituality. That's why he wanted to visit the abbey at night. But, if he wasn't attacked, why is Gemma telling us about the burglary? Does she want us to do something?'

'Quentin himself suggested the police should talk to us about some artefact that was taken.'

'Then, let's get to the police station and find out about it.'

'Not the police station. Gemma's in Watchet, at the chapel over the museum. But, what about this Eggs Benedict I made for you?'

Libby looked at the mess of eggs and slightly curdled sauces on the plate he held out. 'It looks lovely,' she lied, 'but I think we should get moving. I'll eat later.' She grabbed a handful of biscuits and hurried from the kitchen. How was she ever going to tell Max he was the worst cook in the world?

The Watchet museum was cordoned off with police tape, but the stairs leading to the floor above were accessible and the police team was making good use of the chapel.

Amy Fisher, the vicar, bustled about the tiny kitchen and offered cups of tea and Rich Tea biscuits. 'I find these are the best dunkers, don't you?' she murmured to Libby and Max as they arrived.

DC Gemma was talking to Quentin on the other side of the room. The elderly curator looked pale.

'But if he was up welcoming the sun at five o'clock,' Libby reasoned, 'he'll be tired, now.'

'Sunrise was four forty-five,' Max said, checking on his phone, 'and I suppose he was on the Tor all night, partying.'

'With Jemima?' Libby suggested.

They approached Gemma. 'Well,' she said, 'I seem to have missed the real action, last night. I was at Glastonbury.' She yawned. 'I'm about to go off shift, but Mr Dobson, here, wanted you to know what's going on. He thinks the theft is connected to this business of the dead monk.'

Quentin, though pale and tired, seemed not at all embarrassed to be seen wearing the brown robes and multi-striped cloak of a member of the Glastonbury Order of Druids. In fact, he seemed years younger than when Libby last saw him at the Abbey. 'Such a night,' he said, closing his eyes in pure delight at the memory. 'The best solstice I've ever seen – and I've seen many, believe me. They're the highlight of my year. Not a cloud in the sky, last night.'

Even the break-in to his beloved museum had failed to dent his blissful mood. Libby was almost tempted to watch the midsummer sunrise on the Tor for herself, next year.

'I'm sorry,' she said, 'about your museum.'

'Very little damage done, luckily,' he said. 'But would you believe, that American friend of yours had only been talking to me about books yesterday.' He nodded, solemnly.

Max started. 'Reg, you mean?'

'That's the one. He said he'd heard I'm a local expert.' Quentin blinked rapidly, innocently thrilled by the recognition, and Libby could see why Jemima had grown so fond of him. What a shame he had a rival for her affections. Libby hoped he wasn't about to have his elderly heart broken.

Quentin's face fell. 'He knew about the sale of the abbey land and wanted to find out more. I wasn't able to help him – I don't collect books, mostly fossils. I only had two or three old manuscripts.' He sighed. 'They were stolen as well, but our American was very interested in one of the other artefacts – I have a few that were found in the local area.'

'Oh? Max's head shot up. 'What was it?'

'An old box. It's been at the back of the museum for years.'

Libby's breath caught in her throat. The twinkle in the elderly man's eye suggested he was hugging some knowledge to himself. 'Anything interesting in the box?' she asked.

Quentin chuckled. 'I should say so. One of those old prayer books people used to keep in their families. You know the kind of thing? With all the births, marriages and deaths.' A faraway look came over his face. 'I was hoping to bring it to one of the Exham History Society meetings. I could read extracts. I'm sure the members would love it. It's very interesting, especially as it's written in Latin.'

Libby allowed herself a moment to imagine the reactions of the society members to such an idea. The truth was, they came for coffee and cake, a little light gossip and to arrange outings to interesting historical buildings. They preferred any talks to be short and entertaining.

Max was following Quentin's thread. 'And Latin's important because...?'

'The Reformation, dear boy. The break with Rome. The dissolution of the monasteries.'

'Including our abbey, Cleeve.' Max nodded. 'Of course. After the monasteries were destroyed, it was forbidden to hold services in anything other than English. A Latin prayer book would be hidden away and dangerous to own. The owner could be accused of treason under Henry VIII, and again later, under Elizabeth I.'

Quentin continued, 'Now, when we found the skeleton at the abbey, I remembered my box, rescued it from the back of the museum, and showed it to, er...' he blushed like a teenager. 'To Jemima. And to Archie Phillips as well, of course.' He dismissed the librarian with a wave of the hand.

'Go on. What did you find? I can see it was exciting,' Libby pressed.

The elderly man closed his eyes. 'I remember the exact words.' His eyes opened. 'I have a photographic memory, you know.'

'Yes, yes,' Libby jiggled with excitement.

Quentin intoned, with the flair of a magician bringing a rabbit from a hat, 'Tucked into one of the pages of the prayer book was a Bill of Sale for the parcel of land known as the five acres to be sold for £22 5s 6d to Master Wendlebury for his son.'

Libby could hardly contain herself. 'That price – that was the amount the Wendleburys paid for the land, where they built Priory Manor. It must be the same plot, and Master Wendlebury's son could have been one of the monks.'

'The name of the buyer was hard to read, of course, but given the information from the Victorian records, I'm quite sure the name was Wendlebury. It was hard to decipher exactly.'

'That fits with the Victorian book Reg showed us,' Max said. 'Maybe the Wendleburys bought Priory Manor for their son, if he was a monk and lost his home when the abbey was suppressed. So much for monks having no money.'

Quentin said, 'They took a vow of chastity, but they often came from wealthy families. If your son was being thrown out of his abbey, you'd buy a property for him if you could afford it. And if you had any dealings with Sir Richard Rich, you might do a deal.'

'Bribe him, you mean?' Libby suggested. 'Sounds just the kind of thing one of Wendlebury's ancestors would do.'

'But let's not get ahead of ourselves,' Quentin said. He sighed. 'Sadly, we don't know if Wendlebury's ancestor was also our monk, the one we've been calling Bernard.'

Max was nodding. 'But it may be possible to find out.'

Quentin frowned.

'DNA profiling,' Libby explained. 'We can use Wendlebury's DNA to compare with that of our monk. If that's possible, after all this time.'

Max smiled. 'Charlie's ahead of us. She rang while you were at the council meeting to say the AMS results confirm that our monk was indeed alive in the sixteenth century. I meant to tell you last night, but we were so busy worrying about Tom Reeves and his vendetta against Wendlebury that it went out of my head. But, even more interestingly, she also told me she's begun the process of extracting the monk's DNA by crushing the bone into powder and "cleaning up" the contents of the cells.'

Libby made a face. 'Sounds ghastly.'

'The monk won't have felt a thing. But although Charlie now has some of his DNA, she hasn't known of any likely relative for comparison.'

'But now she can find out whether our monk, Bernard, was actually a Wendlebury.' Libby looked with respect at Quentin. 'What a good job you studied the prayer book before it was stolen.'

Quentin looked at his watch. 'Now, if you'll excuse me, I must return home to sleep.'

Libby said, 'Before you go, you need to know about Chesterton Wendlebury.' She told him the bare bones of last night's tragedy, leaving out most of the detail.

'Well,' he said, 'I can hardly believe it. I mean, the chap was a wrong 'un by all accounts – a bit of a snake in the grass, but still, not fair to shoot him.' He gave a huge yawn, looked at his watch and sighed. 'I promised to visit Jemima, today. We have a trip planned to the Somerset Museum.'

As Quentin left, Max grinned at Libby. 'Maybe he's winning the race for Jemima's affections, after all.'

'Well, that's lovely for him. But poor Archie Phillips' nose will be out of joint.'

Max turned serious. 'Reg has certainly been doing his home-work. But I don't believe he broke into the museum – why would he need to, when Quentin had already shown him the prayer book? Chesterton Wendlebury's killer was clearly looking for evidence of the sale, at both Priory Manor and the museum. But we should leave now, and go home. Our children will be arriving later, along with Reg and his new girlfriend. Let's have a lovely time and try to forget all about this dreadful business for a while.'

Libby sighed. 'And we can keep an eye on Reg at the same time – just in case he really is still a suspect.'

For once, Libby planned to use the long dining room at Exham House for the meal, but it needed sprucing up. Mahogany was a beautiful wood for a table, but far too dark for modern taste. She looked around. The sideboard was just as bad. She sighed. This was her house now. She had every right to redecorate and Max had given her free rein over every room except his study, but she'd been reluctant to take over. She brushed imaginary dust from the silver candlesticks on the dresser, tutting quietly, and hid them at the back of the cupboard. Honestly, what had Max been thinking?

She found some of the glass bowls she'd brought from Hope Cottage and tucked candles inside them. At least the garden was full of flowers, so she cut armfuls of peonies, enough to fill every vase she owned.

Searching in the sideboard's drawers, she found an enormous white tablecloth to cover the mahogany monster, and white chair backs. A spot of ironing and they'd transform the chairs.

As she pushed the drawer back in place, something tinkled gently. Intrigued, she upended the drawer's contents. A brightly coloured bag had been hidden at the bottom of the drawer, along with a flat package. Feeling mildly guilty, she opened the bag and peeped inside.

A baby's rattle.

She emptied it out, turned to the other parcel, and pulled out the contents. Baby clothes.

'What are you doing?'

She turned, suddenly embarrassed. 'Sorry. I was just...'

Max was laughing. 'Did you think I was hoarding a dreadful secret? This mysterious monk is getting to you. I bought those things for Sarah's baby. I was going to surprise you.'

Libby's throat felt tight. 'You sentimental old thing,' she said, to hide her feelings. Libby hadn't realised he was so excited about the baby.

'Our first grandchild – of course I'm sentimental. If there's one thing I've learned from you, it's that family comes first.'

'We won't give them to the children tonight. Just in case. You never know, until a baby arrives. Anything could go wrong.'

'For goodness sake,' Max said. 'You have to have something to worry about, don't you? The baby will arrive in his own time, as babies do. Meanwhile, his grandad needs some attention from his wife. Or are you tired of your aging husband?'

'Not quite yet. Although I've had enough of this miserable dining room.'

'Are you talking refurbishment? John Lewis, here we come,' said Max, 'or wherever you go to buy furniture, these days. Now, will you please stop talking.'

* * *

Very much later, Libby straightened her hair and looked at her watch. 'Max, they'll be here in less than two hours and I haven't even started the cooking or ironed the seat covers...'

Max folded his arms. 'There's no need for seat-cover-ironing. Why don't we barbecue? Look at the weather. We don't often get sunshine like this – let's make the most of it.'

Libby flopped into a chair. 'Of course! We have steak and salad and sausages and—'

Max held up a hand. 'We have everything we need, and I'll do the cooking. You can have a rest for once.' He frowned. 'Why are you looking like that?'

'No reason. A barbecue will be wonderful.'

He couldn't go wrong with that, could he?

* * *

By the time their guests turned up, they'd taken extra chairs outside, erected enormous sunshades and found a small table. 'Because Sarah, for one, won't want to stand for hours,' Libby insisted.

When Robert and Sarah arrived, Libby could hardly take her eyes off her daughter-in-law's bump. It seemed enormous. She led her to the sturdiest, most comfortable garden chair and Sarah sank into it with a groan.

'Would another chair be better?' Libby suggested.

Sarah heaved a sigh. 'No, I can't get comfortable these days, no matter where I sit. I have to get up every few minutes and walk around. If I don't, the baby gets bored and kicks me in the ribs. It's been dreadful, today.'

'Feel free to walk around as much as you like,' Max said. 'And we could use a footballer in the family.'

Robert fussed around his wife, trying to make her comfortable with cushions at her back.

She waved him away. 'I'm fine,' she insisted, although she winced. 'Have a drink.'

Joe and Claire arrived moments later, Claire clutching a parcel. 'We might not see you again before the baby arrives, so we've brought this.'

Sarah untied the paper and gasped. 'Did you make this?'

Claire blushed. 'My American mother insisted I learn how to make a quilt.'

'It's just beautiful.' Sarah stroked the quilt that glowed with shades of blue and yellow.

Libby shot a glance at Claire, checking she was all right. Just before Libby's wedding, she'd confessed she was longing for a baby, but Joe wasn't keen.

Claire met Libby's eyes and gave a small shrug. She hadn't convinced Joe, yet.

Max's arm slid around Libby's waist. 'Shall I start the cooking?' he asked.

She gulped. 'Do you need help?'

'Of course not. Nothing could be easier. Where's the petrol—'

The women shrieked in horror, but Joe laughed. 'He always used to say that, when I was a kid.'

'I was the barbecue king at one time, Libby, although I know you don't believe it.' He waved a barbecue fork. 'You think I can't cook, don't you? Well, maybe Eggs Benedict isn't my thing, but burning meat is man's work. Now, you concentrate on making a nice little salad, while we boys take care of the technical business.'

Laughing, Libby left the men squabbling over the best way to light a barbecue and went inside. Bear trotted into the house behind her just as the doorbell rang with the latest arrival.

'Gosh.' Libby threw open the door to Reg, taller and more handsome than ever. But it was his plus-one that had made her gasp.

'Surprise,' Charlie cried, handing her an armful of flowers.

'Reg, you dark horse.' Libby took the huge bottle of champagne from his grasp. 'But I'll take that. Come through, Charlie, and meet the family.' As they walked out into the garden, she hissed in Reg's ear, 'You might have told us.'

Max did a double take. As soon as the introductions were over, he grabbed Reg's arm. 'When did the two of you get together?'

Libby remembered. 'At the abbey, that night. You sat together at the beginning while we were sharing out the kit, didn't you?'

Charlie glanced over her shoulder and grinned. 'He swept me off my feet.'

Libby could imagine it.

Max looked at the sky. 'No rain today. It's time to introduce the beef to the barbecue. Reg, get over here. We all know Americans barbecue all the time, what with the sunshine and all. Come and help. Robert's too busy worrying about Sarah and Joe's hopeless with food.'

'I eat it,' Joe admitted. 'That's as far as it goes.'

'We're just waiting for Ali, now.' There was a hint of irritation in Max's voice. Libby wished her daughter had made the effort to get here on time. She just hoped she'd turn up. She felt a twinge of guilt. Ali had a miscarriage last year. Maybe it was thoughtless, asking her to come while Sarah was about to give birth.

But Ali arrived soon after, with Andy at her side. 'He's here for just a few days.' She smiled, happier than Libby had seen her. While Andy fell into conversation with Reg, Ali revealed an enormous bag full of bright baby clothes for Sarah. 'Yellow and green – like the Brazilian flag,' she pointed out.

Libby caught her eye. It glinted, suspiciously, and Libby knew these were the clothes Ali had bought for her own baby – the one who never came.

Libby swallowed the huge lump in her throat and, with no further cooking to do and the Eton Mess dessert ready in the fridge, forced herself to relax, drink wine and congratulate herself on her family and friends. If only, she thought, Mandy were fit and healthy, and here with them.

43

As the barbecue began to die down, and everyone had eaten more than enough meat and fish, Max announced it was time for dessert. Sarah followed Libby inside the house.

'Are you OK?' Libby asked, as Sarah winced.

'Oh, yes. I've been twinging for days. They're Braxton Hicks – you know, false contractions.'

Libby laid down the Eton Mess. 'Are you sure?'

Sarah's face was chalk white. 'Yes – oof.' She bent over, panting. 'At least—'

Libby waited until the contraction ended. 'How often are they coming?'

'Every now and then. They've been coming all day, but I could hardly feel them. But they're getting worse. Oh dear, here's another—'

At that moment, Ali wandered into the kitchen. 'Mum, can I help—' She broke off and, eyes wide as saucers, watched Sarah gasping for breath. 'How long was that?'

'Not sure,' Sarah gasped. 'Quite long.' She took a breath. 'Oh no...'

Ali moved fast. 'Mum, call an ambulance. The baby's on the way.'

'Can't be…' Sarah grunted. 'Not time…'

'Babies can't tell the time,' Ali said. 'Now, in case the ambulance is late, we need to get you upstairs, if you can make it.'

'Don't… think I can,' she gasped.

'Then, we'll bring towels and things and make you comfortable. Where's best, Mum?'

As Sarah staggered into Max's study, to sit on the floor rug propped on cushions, Ali sent Libby off to organise the rest of the party.

Robert dropped his plastic glass on the ground and bolted inside, followed by Libby and Andy.

'I'm a doctor,' Andy pointed out, and disappeared into the study.

Nothing further happened for what seemed like hours, as the rest of the party stood around uneasily, anxious and excited.

Libby, hardly knowing what to do, made tea that no one drank. 'I wish this ambulance would arrive,' she muttered, listening anxiously to barely audible noises from the study.

Charlie touched her elbow. 'Reg and I will leave you to it. We don't want to get in the way – but you have to promise you'll let us know as soon as the baby comes.'

Libby and Max went to the door to wave them off, watching as they walked down the path, arm in arm. 'They make quite a couple, don't they?' Libby said.

There was no reply.

Surprised, she nudged Max. 'What is it?'

'Look,' Max pointed.

'What? I can't see anything. Oh!'

'For a second,' Max said, 'I thought that was Mandy walking away.'

Libby studied Charlie. Black hair, as dark as Mandy's. Both wore it loose, at shoulder length, although, from the front, Charlie's asymmetrical cut destroyed the similarity. But you couldn't see that from behind. The two women were similar in height. Charlie was more than ten years older than Mandy, but again, from behind, who could tell?

'They could be twins,' Libby said. 'Obviously, that's a type Reg admires—' She broke off, her hands flying to her mouth, as the full implications of the similarity struck her. She turned to face Max. 'What if the attacker made the same mistake? What if he didn't mean to attack Mandy, after all?'

Grimly, Max nodded. 'We've been looking the wrong way. Maybe she wasn't the target. The attacker could have been after Charlie.'

At that moment the midwife, a round, cheerful lady of about forty, arrived, closely followed by the ambulance.

Ali put her head around the study door. 'No time for a trip,' she announced. 'Baby's almost here.'

And, before midnight, Robert appeared in the living room with a bundle in his arms. 'Meet Josh. Our son.'

44

'No wonder we couldn't find a motive.'

It was way past midnight.

Joe and Claire had gone, bemoaning the fact they lived in Hereford, so far away from the new baby. 'My step-nephew – if there is such a thing,' as Joe said.

Ali and Andy had finally gone to bed in one of Exham House's four bedrooms, although Ali had sworn she'd never sleep after such excitement.

Sarah, after talking to her mother on the phone, was asleep in the nicest spare room. Little Josh had taken his first feed and was tucked into the cot Libby had bought. 'In fact,' she'd admitted to Robert, 'I have supplies here of almost everything the baby could need.'

'Well, that's why babies have grannies,' he'd grinned as he yawned, finished the champagne they'd used to wet the baby's head, and joined Sarah upstairs.

Both Libby and Max decided to keep the news that Mandy might have been mistaken for Charlie from the new parents. 'We don't want to spoil their joy,' Max said. 'This is a time they'll never have again. Their first baby.'

'And arriving so fast.' Libby shook her head in wonder. 'It took me a day and a half – and a huge slug of drugs. Lucky Sarah.'

'You're jealous. Wishing Josh was yours?'

'Oh, no. Everyone says grandchildren are your reward for bringing up your children. All the pleasure and none of the sleepless nights.'

They lay back on the sofa.

Max said, 'We really should go to bed.'

'We should. We'll be up early tomorrow. Sarah's mum will be arriving at some ridiculous hour. She would have liked to come tonight, but Sarah put her off. She's dying to see her first grand-child, too.' Libby shook her head. 'But I can't go to bed yet. I need to think this all through.'

Max rested his feet on the coffee table as Libby turned serious.

'We don't know whether the attack on Mandy was meant for her or for Charlie. We've concentrated on the people who were there that night, milling about in the cloister thanks to Ian Smith's stupid prank. The police have talked to Steve and Angela about Mandy's friends, but they couldn't find any motive. Now maybe we know why.'

'We don't know much about Charlie, at all, apart from her professional qualifications.'

'Fancy her looking so similar to Mandy from behind. I can understand the mistake,' Libby said.

'Hm.' Max sounded puzzled.

'Don't you agree?'

'Well, not entirely,' he said, slowly. 'I mean, they weren't dressed like each other at the abbey. Nobody dresses like Mandy, do they?'

'But it was dark, although the sky was full of stars, out there in the countryside.' Libby closed her eyes, reliving the scene. 'Mandy was wearing her scarlet shawl, but Charlie had a green blanket around her shoulders.'

'Not really the same thing. Unless you were colour blind.'

Libby sat up straight. 'Oh dear, that matters, doesn't it? But I can't think why. I don't know anyone who's colour-blind, do you?'

Max shook his head. 'Not consciously, although it's quite a common condition. Especially in men and boys. But I heard it mentioned, not long ago. I wish I could remember where...'

'We should talk to Charlie – tell her about this – and let the police know. She could be in danger, right now.'

'We'll ring her, first thing in the morning,' Max said. 'I think she's safe for now with Reg. He'll keep an eye on her.'

'You don't think...'

'That Reg is the culprit?' He shook his head. 'If he were wanting to kill Charlie, he's had plenty of opportunities. I think, if she's the intended victim, we can take him off the list.'

Libby was biting her thumbnail. 'We haven't worried about Mandy being attacked again while she's been safe in the care of the hospital, but if Charlie's the real target, she needs to stay with Reg at all times until this thing's solved.'

Max rose, pulled Libby to her feet and turned out the lights. 'I think Reg will be happy with that idea. First thing tomorrow, I'll ring DCI Morrison and then Charlie. I know you'll want to concentrate on Robert and Sarah – and their new little boy – until they go home.'

Libby screwed up her face. 'Sarah's mother plans to spend a few days with them in their house, to help them get used to parenthood, so they won't need me after tomorrow morning. If we're right and Charlie's the target, we need to solve all the mysteries - the attack on Mandy, the two burglaries, and

Chesterton Wendlebury's murder - as soon as possible. And, if it's all connected with Bernard, we need to find who killed him. We're right back to the drawing board. I wonder if the police have caught up with Tom Reeves, yet. For my money, he's the most likely suspect, but why he would want to attack Charlie or burgle the museum, I have no idea.'

45

Libby lay awake for hours, thinking, her mind in a spin, and even after she fell asleep, she was plagued by dreams of ghostly monks fighting in the council chambers.

The next morning, though, she woke with a smile on her face. She could hear the baby's cries, quickly subsiding, and slipped along the passage to the spare room, to find Sarah feeding the baby with Robert watching, his face glowing with happiness. Tears rose to Libby's eyes, and she went downstairs to make tea.

Ali was there, moments later.

Libby gave her daughter a warm hug. 'You were wonderful, last night. Especially after...' she paused but was determined to say it, get it out in the open between them. 'After losing your own baby last year.'

Ali smiled. 'I had a long heart-to-heart with Claire. She told me she's longing for a baby, too. She's hoping Josh's arrival yesterday might convince Joe that a baby might not be such a bad idea and, judging by Joe's excitement, I think she's on to a winner.' She hesitated. 'By the way, Andy and I are thinking of getting married.'

Libby dropped her toast and shrieked. 'What?'

'Sorry, is this a bad time?'

'Of course not.' Libby's grin threatened to split her face. 'When did this happen? You didn't say anything at the barbecue.'

'Well, yesterday. After the baby arrived. Andy came over all sentimental and asked if I thought it was a good idea.'

'You mean, he proposed? I can't wait to tell Max.'

Ali's smile was ironic. 'Maybe he'll forgive me for disappearing off to Brazil and making you change your wedding date.'

Libby gulped. 'What has he said?'

'Nothing. Don't worry. But I can tell. He's very quiet when I'm around.'

Libby slipped fresh bread into the toaster. 'Don't worry about it.'

Ali giggled. 'I'm not. I have a plan.'

'Really? What kind of a plan? Nothing crazy, please. We've had enough excitement for a while.'

They were interrupted by the sound of the baby's wails.

Ali frowned. 'It's only an hour since Sarah fed him.'

Libby shrugged. 'Babies can't tell the time. When they're hungry, they need to be fed.'

'Hm. Let's not mention that to Andy. Or Joe.'

Libby swung round. 'You're not trying to tell me you're...'

'Not yet, Mum. That would be just a bit too much, don't you think? But it might not be too long.'

'What about your medical training? Six years in Brazil, isn't it?'

Ali blushed. 'Well, Andy and I have changed our plans. Again. But, it's for the last time, I promise. Andy's starting a new job in England—'

Libby caught her breath, her heart thumping. 'So... so you—'

'Yes, I've managed to transfer to an English university. I'll be going to Leicester in September.'

Libby was speechless.

Ali sniffed. 'What's burning?'

'Oh no. The toast.' Libby ran to the toaster and switched it off.

'We're going to be a nice married couple in a little house, with Andy working in the hospital and me studying and having babies. We're settling down.'

Libby, scraping the black bits off the toast, could hardly take it all in.

Ali said, 'Are you lost for words?'

Libby nodded. She couldn't speak with that lump in her throat.

Just then, Max arrived. 'Good morning, ladies. I hope that toast's not for me—' he broke off. 'What's the matter?'

Libby shook her head, swallowing hard, while Ali explained.

Max sank down onto a stool. 'Good grief.'

Ali said, 'There's one more thing, Max. Will you walk me down the aisle?'

Now, it was Max's turn to be lost for words. He blinked at Ali, a slow smile breaking across his face. 'Do you really want me to?'

'Of course. We're family. I was thinking of asking Robert, but he won't mind. He's a daddy himself, now.'

Libby, recovered, hardly knew whether to laugh or cry. 'Max, I've never seen you blush before.'

'Well, I will be delighted and honoured. I will even buy a new suit.' He grinned at Libby. 'And you can be mother of the bride and wear a posh frock. Maybe one of the ones you bought and then discarded for our wedding? There are at least three hanging in the wardrobe.'

* * *

Finally, when they'd all come down to earth, Max phoned DCI Morrison and Charlie. He found it hard to concentrate. Ali's request had touched him more than he could say. His own daughter had died in a riding accident when she was a teenager. He had never had the chance to walk her down the aisle, and the thought of doing that for Libby's daughter brought him close to tears.

In many ways, Ali was just like Debbie. Both had a knack of driving him crazy with their fierce independence and determination to live their lives in their own style. Ali, like Debbie, was infuriating, but determined and fearless. Libby could be proud of her.

He blew his nose, glad no one had seen him, and rang DCI Morrison.

The DCI, shocked by Max's revelation that Mandy may not have been the attacker's intended victim, agreed he should warn Charlie and tell Reg to stay with her for a while. 'I can't put the manpower I'd like to on to this,' he said. 'There's been no actual threat. It's just supposition, and we're stretched enough covering the Wendlebury murder and the theft from the museum, but I trust your instincts. Can you talk to this Charlie, and try to winkle out any possible motive?'

Tom Reeves had been located in the early hours, back at home and professing horror at the news of Chesterton Wendlebury's death. He would be 'helping the police with our enquiries,' later that day, Morrison said.

The call to Charlie would be difficult. For a long time, Max sat with the phone in his hand, wondering how to phrase things.

He started with the news of the baby.

Charlie congratulated him and asked, 'Do you mind if I put you on speakerphone? Reg has just arrived with coffee and croissants and he'll want to know.'

After filling them in on the baby's arrival, Max moved on to the real reason for his call. It took a while to convince either Charlie or Reg that the attack on Mandy was maybe intended for her.

Reg insisted on Charlie standing, so he could look at her from behind. He said, 'I see what you mean. They could be sisters. And, from behind, there's no telling them apart. Amazing. The two of you aren't related, are you?'

'Not so far as I know. I'm from Yorkshire.'

Max said, 'Well, that may be so, but it leaves us with a whole new area of investigation. We've wondered why anyone might attack Mandy – now we need to look at you instead, Charlie. Any enemies?'

'I can't think of any. Well, no one who'd want to hurt me seriously. I won the university tennis tournament last year, which upset a few colleagues, but I can't think that would lead to murder. And I didn't know most of the people at the ghost hunt.'

'What about academic rivals?' Max asked. 'Anyone who wanted your job?'

'Plenty, but there are always disappointed candidates and jobs in other universities. I haven't received any threats. Everyone was very kind and welcoming when I started here a year ago. On the surface, at least. There's professional jealousy, because we all want to have more papers published than our colleagues, of course...' She paused, as though mentally running through her colleagues. 'No, I can't think of anybody.'

Reg said, 'Isn't it true that it must have been one of the people attending the ghost-hunting shindig who was responsible for the attack?'

Charlie disagreed, 'Probably, but not definitely. Access to the gatehouse is not restricted – it was designed so the monks could give out food, remember, without opening the gates. There's a wall around the abbey, but it's ruined and easy enough to climb over. Anyone could get into the outdoor areas, although spaces like the refectory, the dormitory and the exhibition areas are locked at night. They were left open especially for our ghost hunt, thanks to Rosalind.'

Reg mused aloud, 'The cloister's easily accessible, but if the note went into Mandy's pocket while we all milled around, thanks to that idiot of a police officer, we would have noticed an interloper.'

'So,' Max sighed, 'we really are looking at someone we know.'

'That's a horrible thought,' Charlie said.

Max went on, 'And, it leaves me wondering whether there's something about our monk, his murder all those years ago, and your work that's at the bottom of all this.' He asked, 'Is there anyone who'd want to stop you looking more carefully into Bernard's death?'

Charlie sighed. 'Can't think of anyone. Everyone I speak to is fascinated by it and wants to know more. If this is all to do with the bones we found, maybe I should contact colleagues in other universities, see if anyone has ideas. Parts of skeletons are often found after floods or landslips.'

'Meanwhile,' Reg said, 'I'll stick here with Charlie. One of the advantages of being an ex-basketball player is I make a decent bodyguard.'

Max agreed. 'And, Libby and I will keep thinking. She may have one of her bright ideas. Although, she's got a lot on her mind, at the moment.'

46

HOSPITAL

The next few days passed quietly. Libby, suitably certificated, was allowed to take Bear to visit Mandy.

At first Mandy lay silently, not noticing he was there. 'Tired,' she muttered.

Libby shot a questioning look at Steve, who'd hardly left his girlfriend's side.

With a glance at Mandy as she settled down to sleep, he took Libby and Bear outside. He seemed to have aged many years.

'She's still having trouble with her speech,' he said, clearly fighting to hold back the tears. 'Something to do with the area of her brain where there was bleeding.'

Libby, shocked, asked, 'Will it get better?'

Steve bit his lip. 'The doctors are hopeful. They say that with someone as young and healthy as Mandy, they expect some progress over the next few weeks.'

'Weeks?' Libby gasped. 'You're joking. Will she have to stay in hospital?'

'Apparently not. At the moment she's very tired and sleeps a lot, but she doesn't need any more surgery. She sees the speech therapist every day, and he's going to give us a lot of advice and exercises, and when she's stronger, she's going home to stay with her mum in Bristol.'

Libby felt sick. 'We thought bringing Bear to see her might help.'

'It will. And we do singing with her – she's able to remember the words to songs and that cheers her up. But she still can't talk about that night.'

'Can't, or doesn't want to?' Libby wondered.

'We don't know, really.'

Libby and Bear walked back towards Mandy's room.

Steve hovered in the doorway. He gestured at Mandy. 'I try to talk to her. They tell me she still has trouble understanding what I say, but that's getting better. The therapist says that's a good sign and I have to use simple sentences to help her. Oh,' he stopped. 'Did you send her this?' He pointed to a large, flowery *Get Well* card.

Libby looked inside it. There was no signature. 'No, it's not mine,' she said. She nodded at a jokey card on the table. 'That's mine. It's funny the sender didn't sign this card though.'

'Oh, well, I expect we'll find out.'

Mandy had napped for a few moments, but as they'd walked into the room, she woke up again. 'Hello,' she said, sounding for a second just like the old Mandy.

Libby struggled to keep a smile on her face. 'Look who's come to see you,' she said.

Mandy grinned, noticing the dog for the first time. 'B-Bear!' Her face lit up.

'He was pining for you,' Libby smiled. 'We all are.'

Mandy reached over to scratch Bear's ears.

Reluctantly, Libby decided she should tell Mandy the truth

about the attack. It might put her young friend's mind at rest to know she wasn't the intended victim.

She took a moment, planning how to explain it in simple sentences, as Steve had suggested.

Mandy had stopped petting Bear and was looking at Libby suspiciously. 'What is it?'

'Mandy,' Libby said, 'remember the abbey?'

Mandy frowned, as though thinking. 'I remember.'

Libby went on, 'I think it was all a mistake.'

'A mistake?' Mandy repeated, looking puzzled.

Libby pointed to the side of her head. 'The bang on your head.'

Mandy nodded.

'The attack was meant for Charlie.'

Mandy repeated the words. 'Charlie. For Charlie.' Suddenly, her face cleared. 'For Charlie? Not me?'

'That's right. Someone wanted to hurt Charlie. You were a mistake.'

Mandy thought about that, her eyes narrowed. 'A mistake. Acci-accident?' she said, at last, and a smile spread across her face.

Libby wanted to shout with joy. 'Yes, it was just an accident. No one wanted to hurt you.'

There would be time to explain properly when Mandy was better. For the moment, she seemed relieved to know she wasn't the intended victim.

She flopped back against her pillows, murmuring, 'An accident.' She let her hand drop onto Bear's head. 'Just an accident, Bear,' she said, and laughed.

* * *

'It was terrible to see her like that,' Libby told Max when she got home that afternoon. 'But Bear helped, and she understood that the attack wasn't meant for her. She was thrilled. I think she's been terrified, not understanding what happened to her or why. And she couldn't tell anyone because she couldn't put her fears into words.' She felt tears prickling her eyes. 'Steve was so relieved. Poor lad, he looked like a ghost, himself. He says it's still going to take a long time for her to recover fully, but it was a big step forward.'

Max went to the fridge and pulled out a tray of ice cubes and the gin bottle. 'That's the first bit of good news we've had about Mandy since the attack, so I think a small celebration is in order.' He unscrewed the bottle. 'Although, I hate to spoil things, but even though Mandy seems to be out of danger – not that we're even sure about that – Charlie could still be in trouble. If that attack on Mandy was someone trying to kill Charlie, they failed. What's to stop them trying again?'

'You're right, of course.' Libby blew out her cheeks and puffed the air from her mouth. 'This case is all one step forward and two steps back. If only we could find the link between our monk and Charlie. I'm sure that's at the centre of all this.'

Max handed her a gin and tonic. 'Maybe this will help you think.'

'Put me to sleep, more likely,' she said.

Max's phone rang. He answered and his jaw dropped. 'It's Charlie.'

'Put her on speaker,' Libby hissed.

'I've heard from one of my colleagues,' Charlie was saying. 'Some sixteenth century bones disappeared from their museum a couple of weeks ago, just before Bernard was discovered. I've been ringing round everyone in the business – there aren't too many of us. Derek, up in Manchester, said they lost the bones and thought it was some idiotic clerical error or a stupid prank – you know, students moving them. You see, they aren't the most exciting bones. There's nothing special about them. They came from the graveyard of a monastery in Scotland during one of those TV digs.'

'*Time Team*?' Max suggested.

'Something like that. And the age of the bones is similar to Bernard's. Derek's wondering if the thief put them in the Washford River – although why they would do that we have no idea.'

Max's eyes met Libby's. 'That's crazy.'

'Exactly. But, the timing's right. Derek's set disappeared and ours showed up in the river a few days later. I described them and Derek said they might be the same – although he didn't know about the blue colouring.' She chuckled down the line. 'I'm feeling pretty smug about that. I've met Derek a few times, at conferences and so on, and he's a great know-all. He'll be kicking himself because he missed that. Especially when he sees my article in the journal.' She sounded excited. 'Anyway, he says he can't wait to see the bones, check they're the same ones and take them back. He's coming over tomorrow. So do you and Libby want to come? I may have the DNA results by then, so we'll know if Bernard and Chesterton Wendlebury were related. Although, if the bones don't belong in Somerset, the Wendlebury connection disappears.'

'Libby and I will be there.' Max clicked off the phone.

Libby said, 'This puts a whole new spin on things. Someone went to the trouble of stealing bones, bringing them all the way from Manchester to Somerset, and planting them in the stream. Why on earth would they do such a thing, and what connection would it have to the attempt on Charlie's life?'

'I've no ideas,' Max said, 'but a lot of questions.'

'Me too.'

Max turned up the air conditioning in the car on the way to Bristol. 'This weather's getting too much for me. I like a few days of sun, but this year it's getting to be a bore, and I'm starting to long for the autumn.'

Libby agreed, 'Big coats, woolly jumpers, log fires, and walks in the frosty air. Still, it's past the solstice. The nights are drawing in, now. It won't be too long.'

'I think this weather's likely to break, soon. It's so humid. It makes every movement difficult.' He overtook a series of caravans warily, for one was swaying dangerously out of its lane. 'At least we know Bernard's room will be cool. The temperature's perfectly controlled to prevent skeletons deteriorating.'

When they arrived at the university, Charlie's colleague had not yet arrived. Charlie was piling mugs and cutlery on a tray in the tiny room next to the monk's temporary resting place. 'This place is a tip. I'd be embarrassed for a researcher from another university to see it. Rory usually keeps it tidy, but he hasn't been in for a couple of days. Too busy with end-of-year parties, I suppose, although he's planning to show his face today. And in case you're worried, Reg hasn't left my side since your phone call. He dropped me off this morning and he's picking me up about four o'clock. We reckon I'm perfectly safe at uni – if anyone was going to attack me here, they would already have had plenty of opportunities.' Charlie loaded more cups on the already full tray. 'If we find the bones came from somewhere else, I'm afraid it means they don't belong to our Cleeve Abbey monk Bernard at all.'

Just then, Rory's head poked around the door.

Charlie said, 'We were just talking about the Manchester bones. I wonder why anyone would want to move them?'

Rory shrugged, scratching his head until the hair stood up in bright spikes. 'No idea. But it would be a shame, given all the work we've put in to Bernard's history.'

Libby commiserated. 'The History Society will be devastated. And it would wipe out all our theories about the connection between finding Bernard and the attack on Mandy—Watch out.' She lunged forward to steady Charlie's tray. 'That cup nearly went on the floor.'

Charlie sighed, 'Sorry. Rory, could you sort the rest of this mess out while I show Bernard to Libby?'

As Rory took the tray, Charlie led the others into the peace of Bernard's room.

'Now, what were we saying? Oh yes, Bernard possibly not coming from Cleeve Abbey at all. Well, it will be a blow, I can't deny but I'll still get my paper out of all this. Unfortunately, it may not be as academic as I originally intended, but I think I can find a different audience that will give me even better exposure.'

'What kind of audience?' Max enquired.

'There's the paranormal aspect, you see. The ghost hunting. I'm following that up with Rosalind, who tells me you're planning a late afternoon trip to the abbey today. I'd like to tag along if you don't mind.'

'What's Rosalind up to now?' Libby asked.

Before Charlie could explain, a thump on the door interrupted them.

Rory poked his head around to say, 'He's here.'

'Morning, all.' A gangly man of middle age, with a beard and scruffy, long hair and rumpled clothes was in the tea room. 'I'm gasping for a gallon of water and a cup of coffee. My air-conditioning broke down halfway through the journey.' He paused, as though detecting an uncomfortable atmosphere in the room. 'Anything wrong?'

'Nothing at all,' Charlie said, with a small shrug. 'Welcome to Bristol.' She made the introductions as she poured coffee and glasses of ice water from the new supplies Rory had brought. 'We're hoping you can shed some light on these bones. Libby and Max, here, have been helping to find out what happened to the monk, because we thought he came from the local abbey. But, if you're right, he's not from Somerset at all.'

'Well,' Derek said, cheerfully, downing his coffee in one gulp, reaching into his briefcase and waving a thick file. 'Let's have a look at the poor fellow. I've brought all the information, although you've probably already had a good look at it online. Still, nothing like the real thing, is there? Where is he?'

Along with Charlie and Rory, he spent the next ten minutes poring over Bernard's bones. Libby and Max stood quietly, listening.

Libby muttered, 'Do you understand what they're saying?'

'About one word in ten,' Max admitted.

Soon, Derek was shaking his head. He'd put a sheet of something that looked to Libby like an X-ray up on the backlit board on one side of the room. Charlie added another and they spent a long time comparing the two.

Finally, Derek turned. 'Sorry, that's not our man,' he said.

'Thought so,' Rory pumped the air.

Charlie shook her head. 'Well. Fancy that. It seems Derek's students were just playing a stupid prank on the university.'

Derek groaned. 'Every year group tries something. They all think they're being original. I suppose our monk will turn up somewhere in a day or two, as part of the leaving celebrations. He'll probably pop up in a student's bed, and we'll have to deal with hysterical undergraduates and furious parents.'

Max said, 'Or in a TikTok video.'

Libby said, 'Aren't these ancient bones valuable?'

Derek sighed. 'Only to us, as teaching aids. There are plenty of them available. Most are reburied properly once they've been analysed, but we keep an occasional specimen for teaching purposes. We try to treat them with respect, but it's hard to convince the students.'

'I suppose,' Libby noted, 'that this explains the discrepancy over the blue dye. You didn't notice it, Derek, because it wasn't there.'

He let out a roar of laughter. 'If I'd trusted my own judgement, I'd have saved myself the journey, today. Still, always nice to come down south, see what the natives of Bristol are up to. And good to meet you all,' he added hastily.

Charlie said, 'The least I can do is offer you lunch in town.' She turned to Libby and Max. 'Will you join us?'

'Thanks, but no,' Libby said. 'We'll see you later at the abbey.' She broke off, biting her lip. No need to broadcast the news of the attack on Mandy to Derek, no matter how friendly he seemed. As they left, she said to Max, 'I reckon Reg has some competition there. Did you notice the spark between those two?'

'I'd like to say, what nonsense,' Max admitted, 'but I think you're right. He came a long way on a wild goose chase. I think he used it as an excuse to see Charlie. And he wasn't wearing a wedding ring.'

'That doesn't mean too much, these days.' Libby shot an automatic glance at the shiny new gold band on her own left hand. 'But, if his hair and clothes are anything to go by, no one's looking after him. Did you see the hole in his sleeve?'

'Reg may have a rival, then. Maybe Charlie won't be wife number four, after all.'

'More to the point,' Libby said. 'What are Charlie and Rosalind cooking up together for later today?'

48

Charlie had already arrived at the abbey with Reg when Max and Libby drove into the car park, locked the car and crossed the road over the river where Bernard's bones had appeared.

Max asked Charlie, 'Has Derek gone back to Manchester?'

'Who's Derek?' Reg asked.

Charlie's eyes shot daggers at Max. 'My colleague from Manchester. I told you.'

'Ah. The ancient professor of bones.'

Max covered his derisive grunt with a cough. It seemed Charlie had provided a carefully edited description of Derek.

'What is it?' Charlie looked at him with narrowed eyes, but Max kept his face straight

'Nothing. Let's go into the abbey and see if the dogs can find anything spooky.'

'Before we do,' Charlie was grinning, her perfect teeth gleaming white, 'I have news.'

Libby's head turned. 'News? About Bernard the monk?'

Charlie was nodding. 'I had an email this afternoon, when I got back to the university after, er...' she hesitated, doubtless remembering she'd been having lunch with a man who wasn't Reg. 'After lunch,' she continued, not meeting Max's eyes. 'Our monk is not related to your friend Chesterton Wendlebury after all.'

'Oh,' Libby sounded deflated. 'Bernard wasn't a Wendlebury. That blows all our ideas out of the water.'

Reg, who'd been watching with a slightly confused expression, said, 'So, we're no further ahead?'

'Not exactly,' Charlie said. 'While my colleagues were looking at the DNA sequence, they matched it to others in their data bank. Do you remember, some years ago, a skeleton turned up in the caves in Cheddar, and all the local people gave DNA samples?'

Max screwed his face up, remembering. 'I do. It was before you came to Exham, Libby. They discovered the caveman was related to a teacher that still lived in the area.'

Charlie was grinning. 'Well, the DNA samples were still on the database – and one of them gave us a match for Bernard.'

Libby held her breath as Charlie paused.

'Go on,' Max said. 'Don't keep us in suspense.'

'Bernard is a distant relative of Tom Reeves.'

Libby groaned. 'So, our monk Bernard, who wrote the Tudor equivalent of "we've been robbed" on the manuscript, was a Reeves. We're back to Tom – and with another chunk of circumstantial evidence against him. His ancestor, our monk, thought the family was robbed when the Wendleburys bought the land from the Court of Augmentations. I bet it was something to do with bribery. Maybe the Reeves family had already paid something to Sir Richard Rich but the Wendleburys gazumped them and killed our monk to shut him up.'

Max shook his head. 'Things are looking even worse for Tom Reeves, now.'

Charlie bent to stroke Bear. 'I've told your DCI Morrison. He didn't sound at all excited.'

'He never does,' Max said. 'But he'll be on to it – it's another reason for the chip on Tom's shoulder. Let's think it all through.' He closed one eye, trying to get his tangled thoughts in order. 'Tom's family have harboured a grudge against the Wendleburys for many years. In addition, Tom's fiercely opposed to house building that he thinks will ruin the area. That's another reason for him to hate the Wendleburys.'

Charlie and Libby were both nodding. Charlie said, 'That makes sense, so far.'

Max continued, 'When the Wendleburys put plans forward for new housing at the manor, Tom lost control completely. After the fight at the council, he went to the manor to look for evidence that the Wendleburys cheated the Reeves family, but Chesterton was there. Tom was startled, and shot him. I think that's the case the police will make, unless Tom has a brilliant alibi for the night of the killing. And, if they find the gun belongs to Tom, Chesterton's death will be an open-and-shut case of at least manslaughter, if not murder.'

Libby said. 'But even if Tom killed Chesterton, why would he try to kill Charlie?'

Charlie shivered. 'Maybe to stop me investigating?'

'But, why would that matter to him?' Libby groaned. She turned to look at the abbey, its old ruins glowing peacefully in the afternoon sun. 'It doesn't feel right. In any case, I don't think Tom's the type to pass secret notes, lure his victims to quiet locations or break into museums. He's not that subtle. He's what my granny used to call all mouth and trousers; shouting and waving his fists around, but totally ineffective. I think our killer is quieter, more intelligent, and craftier than Tom, and has a reason to attack Charlie that we don't yet know about'

Max said, 'Let's leave it for tonight. Charlie's safe enough with us here, if she really is a target, and we can leave Tom Reeves to the police.'

Libby agreed. 'Let's see if the dogs will ferret out any more evidence of ghosts, as Rosalind hopes. I'm afraid she sees this whole business as an opportunity to publicise her TV programme.'

Charlie opened her mouth, but before she could speak a car drove into the car park.

'And here's Rosalind herself, right on cue,' Max said.

The small group formed a circle on the grass at the abbey, just outside the gatehouse. Reg held Charlie's hand. Rosalind joined them, puffing and panting as she struggled with a massive black tripod. A pair of cameras hung round her neck.

Max said, 'We didn't know you were planning to film today. Is this for your TV show? Because if it is, you really should have mentioned it when you asked us along. We don't want to be filmed.'

'And we won't agree to using the attack on Mandy for profit,' Libby added.

Rosalind had the grace to blush. 'Well,' she said, 'no one has to be part of the filming. I plan to do a short piece to camera in the cloister – it's such a beautiful location. I'll just talk about the monk, not Mandy.' She fiddled with a camera case. 'Charlie and I talked about it – Charlie will cover the anthropology – what she's discovered from the bones – while I provide the historical and ghost footage. No one else needs to be involved.'

Libby raised her eyebrows at Charlie. 'I didn't know your collaboration had got so far.'

Charlie blushed and looked at her feet. 'I told you I was looking at other options as well as my academic paper.'

Reg frowned and dropped Charlie's hand. 'You didn't tell me you were planning this. We all feel pretty protective about Mandy.'

Charlie reddened, and Libby said, 'We can't stop you two, but please keep me out of it—'

'And me,' Max said, 'and don't say anything about Mandy.'

'Of course not,' Rosalind said, setting up her tripod and avoiding his eyes. 'But may I film your dogs if they find anything interesting?'

Max shared a glance with Libby. 'I suppose so,' he said. 'They won't care.'

The five humans and two dogs made their way across the grass towards the gatehouse. Max held Shipley's lead, leaving Libby in charge of Bear.

Libby muttered in Max's ear, 'Do you trust Rosalind?'

'Not in the slightest. I'd rather trust Shipley to ignore the scent of rabbits, and I don't know how far this collaboration between Rosalind and Charlie has gone. Rosalind's a manipulator – look how she persuaded us all to come on the original ghost hunt. Is Charlie walking into something she'll regret? She'll need to make sure any contract she signs is watertight.'

Libby squeezed his hand. 'What did you say?'

He laughed. 'Charlie and the contract?'

'No, before that. About Rosalind.' She shook her head. 'No, I'm making connections that aren't there. Forget it.'

What had he said out of the ordinary? Max tried to remember. Rosalind was a manipulative woman, that was true, but according to Libby, the History Society had been keen on the ghost hunt. They'd all been looking forward to meeting Cleeva Clapp's good monks.

Dusk was falling slowly. Max stood still, letting Shipley sniff around his feet. The river behind him gurgled quietly, interrupted only by the call of the rooks as they made their way back to the trees. Could he feel a presence here?

No. There was nothing but peace and calm.

He walked on, to the gatehouse, where the heat of the day had been trapped inside the mellow stone walls. Shipley hesitated at the south front and looked back at Max. 'Go on,' Max encouraged. 'See what you can find,' and he followed Shipley inside.

The small group stood close together.

Libby touched the wall. 'This is the spot where Mandy's attacker jumped out at her.' She shivered.

Charlie said, 'How is Mandy? Any better?'

Libby nodded. 'A little. She's talking more, just a few words, so far, but the doctors are keen to let her go home. Unfortunately, she still can't tell us anything about the attack. That night's a blank to her. We're hoping she'll remember, soon, when she's stronger. The police plan to show her pictures of the people at the ghost hunt again to see if she recognises her attacker, but it's all a waiting game. What's that?' Libby pointed at a sign on the wall.

Charlie scanned it as Rosalind filmed. 'This part of the abbey used to be accessible from the outside even when the gates were closed. The monks handed out food and drink to the poor, here,' Charlie said.

She'd be a good TV presenter, Max decided. Maybe they were being hard on both her and Rosalind. Everyone had to make a living.

Libby was keeping well out of Rosalind's way. Max smiled to himself. His wife's curiosity was too strong to let her opt out of any investigation, no matter how distressing, but she'd hate to see herself on screen.

She stroked the stones, 'It's shocking to think of an attempted murder in such a peaceful place that was intended only for good works.'

'Imagine all the things the monks saw, though,' Reg said. 'The medieval years were tough, especially for the poor and sick. Imagine the illnesses that were rife back then; leprosy, smallpox, plague. And the monasteries provided the hospitals.'

Charlie was nodding, 'Then, there were constant wars and local rivalries. Probably several killings, too. I bet our Bernard wasn't the only one murdered in the chaos when monastery land came up for grabs.'

Shipley was standing in a corner of the gatehouse, sniffing at the walls. 'What is it?' Max asked. 'Can you smell something?'

Bear joined Shipley.

Max raised his eyebrows. 'They can both sense something, but who knows what? Perhaps he can just smell other dogs, here. Hundreds must visit the abbey every year.'

Libby's face fell. 'I was hoping the dogs might give us a clue, but there's nothing here for them to find.'

At least there were no signs of violence in the gatehouse. The police had finished examining the small space, leaving it to its air of ancient serenity.

Charlie was examining the walls with evident professional interest. 'The stone's mostly in good order,' she said. 'There's even some of the old plaster and limewash left. Fascinating.'

Libby said, 'We're not going to find anything here. Let's go on to the main buildings.'

'I'll follow in a minute,' Charlie said. 'I'd like to have a closer look since we think Bernard knew about this theft. There may be a clue, here, where members of the public used to come.'

Max and Shipley led the way across the grass, towards the square of buildings surrounding the cloister.

Libby said, 'I'd almost lost interest in our monk. A murder all those years ago doesn't seem to matter too much now.'

Reg walked with them, leaving Charlie and Rosalind in the gatehouse. 'Charlie's sure keen on her career.' He looked troubled. 'I mean, that's fine with me, but I don't appreciate the way she's using you guys and the attack on Mandy for her own ends. She's a touch like Rosalind – a bit self-centred. Friends are more important than papers and TV programmes. At least, they are to me. I can't talk for other folks.'

Libby stopped, suddenly motionless, her eyes looking far away at nothing.

'What's wrong?' Max said. 'You've had an idea, haven't you? I recognise that face you're making.'

She blinked and refocused. 'I'm not sure. It's just a thought. All this talk of careers...' Bear tugged at his lead. 'Sorry, Bear. Ignore me, Max, it's probably nothing.'

She walked away, Reg and Max following with the dogs.

'I'd like to film the walk along the alleyway, opening out to the place where the chapel used to stand,' Rosalind called. 'Could you help me carry this tripod to the cloister, Reg?'

Reg shook his head but returned to the gatehouse to help. Soon, he emerged with the tripod on his shoulder and staggered past Libby and Max, muttering about useless film directors.

As Libby and Max reached the corner of the alley, Max looked back. 'Where are Charlie and Rosalind?' he asked.

'Still inside the gatehouse, I suppose,' Libby said. She stopped, suddenly. 'Max.' She grabbed his arm. 'Max, I've just remembered. In Rosalind's garden, she told us about the flowers, said the colours were random because—' she waited, looking expectantly at Max.

He took a moment to think. 'Because her husband's "terrible with colours".'

'And Mandy's attacker mistook her red cloak for Charlie's green blanket.'

Libby began to run. 'Colour blind. The attacker was colour blind. Was it her husband who can't see colours or Rosalind?' She broke off, running towards the gatehouse.

Max followed. 'And Rosalind's alone with Charlie—'

'He broke off as a shotgun blast echoed around the abbey.

'Charlie?' Max cried. He threw down the dog's leads and let them run ahead to the gatehouse, towards the sound of the shot.

Behind, still in the cloister, Reg dropped the tripod, shouted, and followed, his long legs covering the ground like a sprinter until he caught Max.

Together, the two men charged through the inner archway of the gatehouse.

By the time Libby arrived, Charlie was leaning against the stones, Reg at her side, but Max was chasing Rosalind out of the south arch, towards the car park across the lane.

Charlie muttered, 'There's a gun – it... it hit me—' A patch of red showed on the shoulder of her jacket. 'I don't think it did much damage...' she muttered, twisting her head to look at her arm.

Libby ran after Max. 'Max, stop, she's got a gun—'

Rosalind had crossed the bridge and was running up the lane. But she had no gun that Libby could see. Had she dropped it?

Shipley caught up with Rosalind but ran straight past, without pausing, Bear close behind, and Max to the rear. Libby realised someone else was there, someone running ahead, aiming for the corner of the lane, running for his life, but Shipley was gaining on him.

The figure turned, stopped and raised the gun.

'Rory!' Rosalind shrieked. 'Drop that now.'

Rory hesitated. In that split second, Shipley leapt, snarling, and fastened his teeth on Rory's gun arm.

Bear growled, menacingly, hackles raised.

Rory screamed, 'Call these dogs off.'

He shouted and squirmed, struggling to shake Shipley off, but the dog's jaws were clamped tight. 'He'll have my arm off.'

'He will, unless you keep still,' Max had arrived.

'I'll have the law on you—' Rory broke off, and his voice changed to a whine. He looked at Rosalind. 'Make him stop, Mum,' he pleaded.

'Mum?' Libby gasped.

Rosalind sank to the ground, her hands over her face, sobbing, and Max ordered Shipley to let go of Rory's arm

The student stood poised for flight, his head swivelling, eyes questing for an escape route.

'It's no good running,' Max pointed out, cheerfully. 'Shipley will catch you again – and maybe he'll take your arm off, next time.' He picked up the shotgun, broke it over his arm, and retrieved Shipley's lead. The spaniel, still excited, tried to pull away and chase Rory some more. 'Leave him, Shipley,' Max said.

The panic died from Rory's eyes. Now they were narrow, calculating. 'I didn't mean to shoot Charlie.' He spread his hands in a caricature of innocence. 'Honest. I just walked in to the gatehouse and she screamed at me, made me jump—' He swallowed. 'Mum? Tell them I didn't mean to do it.'

Max and Reg, gripping Rory's arms, walked him back down the road and into the gatehouse, while Libby followed with the dogs.

Rory muttered under his breath, mouthing a string of obscenities.

Rosalind faced him, her face drained of colour. 'What have you done?'

His laugh rang hollow. 'Nothing. I did nothing. Charlie screamed and the gun went off. I didn't mean it.'

Rosalind whispered. 'But why, Rory, after all we've done for you?'

'Done for me?' His face twisted. 'You let me down, Mum, just like all the rest.' He pointed at Charlie. 'You're no better than her. She's a thief, and she's been planning to steal my work. All so she can write that paper she's planning. She's like you – all you care about is yourselves and your stupid, selfish careers.'

Charlie gasped.

'I did all the work,' Rory shouted. 'And you want to take all the credit. You hardly even noticed I was there – just "Rory, make the tea" and "Rory, photocopy my reports."' He turned to his mother, his eyes blazing. Libby's blood ran cold at the hatred distorting his face. 'As for you – my own mother – you never cared about me. You even left me out of your pathetic film.'

Max tightened his grip.

'I've called the police,' Reg said, 'and an ambulance is on its way for Charlie.'

'I really don't need one,' Charlie insisted. 'The shot just grazed my shoulder.'

'Lucky for you,' Reg towered over Rory threateningly.

Rory's lip curled. 'Look at you all,' he said. 'So smug, the lot of you. Especially my mother.' His lip curled. 'You and your second career. Didn't include me, did you? And nor did she,' with a jerk of his head towards Charlie. 'It was me that saw the blue stains on the monk's tooth, not her. I made the discovery of my life and she stole it, writing it up for some stuck-up journal, so she'd get all the credit.'

Charlie gasped. 'And for that, you tried to kill me? You're crazy.'

Rory's eyes glittered like a trapped animal's as he growled through clenched teeth. 'Say that again and you'll be sorry.'

'He can't help it,' Rosalind said, desperation in her voice. 'He's always been a bit different from other boys. Sensitive. He gets too upset about things – like Freddy's death.'

'What?' Reg interrupted. 'Who the heck's Freddy?'

'Yeah,' Rory said. 'You're right. I am different from you – because you're a stupid, ignorant woman. Uncle Tom and Freddy - they understood. You have to stand up for yourself in this world. Take what you deserve, because no one will help you.'

Libby shuddered. Rory, the quiet, enthusiastic student, was a monster. 'What about Chesterton Wendlebury?' she asked. 'What did he have to do with you?'

Rory snorted. 'Stupid old git. He thought his family was better than ours. Freddy told me the whole story. The Wendleburys stole Priory Manor. Freddy should have lived there. Uncle Tom used to tell Freddy he'd get his own back on the Wendleburys, one day. Freddy did some research, back when we shared a flat in London. He was always in the library and he uncovered the truth. It was just like Uncle Tom told him. The Wendleburys bribed officials to get their hands on the land where they built Priory Manor. The Reeves had already paid for it, but the Court took the Wendlebury money and gave it to them.'

Libby nodded, 'The Reeves were gazumped? The Court broke its promise?'

'Not exactly hard to believe,' Max said.

'No wonder Tom was so angry about the housing estate plans,' Libby said. 'Although he didn't know a Wendlebury probably murdered his ancestor to keep the secret.'

Rory was weeping. 'Freddy wasn't really bothered, but when he died…' He sobbed so hard the listeners had to strain to understand, 'when he died, I went on with the research.' He looked up, his eyes suddenly sharp. The tears had dried. 'Uncle Tom kept a couple of guns on the farm – old shotguns, he'd had them for years. Anyway, I thought Wendlebury would have evidence at the Manor. The Wendleburys always thought themselves a cut above the rest of us. I knew they'd have kept something to show how long they've lived there and so I broke in. I thought I'd give him a fright. I thought he was out, at the planning meeting, but it ended earlier than I expected.'

'Because of the fight,' Libby said, 'between your uncle and Chesterton Wendlebury.'

Rory shrugged, and wiped his face on his sleeve. 'I used the gun to shoot my way in.' He showed no sign of remorse for what he'd done. 'Wendlebury appeared and swore at me, so I popped him one. I didn't kill him. It was his own fault he fell down the stairs.'

Rosalind wailed, 'You stupid, stupid boy. As if Freddy would have wanted you to kill anyone. Your cousin was a lovely, gentle boy.'

Libby looked Rosalind in the face. 'Did you see Rory that night at the abbey, on his way to the gatehouse? Your records stopped at ten thirty, but we were there until after midnight.'

Rosalind's lip trembled. 'I wasn't sure. I mean, at the time, I thought it was one of the monks. Then, later, I started to wonder – but I couldn't believe Rory would do such a thing. And, I didn't know for sure.'

Libby's face was close to hers. 'Because you kept your mouth shut, your son went on to kill Chesterton. I hope you're proud of yourself.'

'And,' Max added, as tears trickled down Rosalind's cheeks, 'the police will be very interested to hear that you withheld evidence.'

There had never been a better attendance than at the next History Society meeting. Motivated by a mix of curiosity and sympathy for Chesterton Wendlebury, and anger at the attempt on Mandy's life, no one wanted to miss the details of Rory's arrest and his relationship with Rosalind.

'I'm so sad for Chesterton,' Angela said. 'He wasn't a likeable man and he was a petty criminal, but he'd served his time in prison. He didn't deserve to be killed just when things were going better for him.'

'You can never tell who might cross the line into murder.' Marjorie, holding her husband William's hand, gave a small shiver. She'd had her own brush with an attempted murder.

William said, 'Is this Rory character crazy, going around attacking people? What will the police do with him?'

'I'm afraid,' Libby said, 'he's a very scary person. He had a chip on his shoulder the size of a boulder, but he doesn't seem to care whether people die or not. He was close to his young cousin Freddy – or, as close as he would get to anyone. But he introduced Freddy to drugs and they led to Freddy's death. Rory hasn't shown any sign of remorse about that. It seems he let the injustice done to the Reeves family all those years ago fester in his mind, feeding his sense of grievance. He thinks everyone's out to cheat him, including his own mother, Rosalind.'

Gemma, promoted to Acting Detective Sergeant, had come to today's meeting to share as much as she could without prejudicing the case the police were building against Rory. She was, Libby realised, fast becoming an honorary member of the History Society.

She said, 'Rory and Freddy were sharing a flat in London when Rory introduced him to drugs. Then, when Freddy tried to come off them without help, he suffered some kind of paranoia – it's quite common when people go "cold turkey" – and ran into the road, trying to get away from some horror conjured up by his own mind.'

Libby took up the tale. 'Winifred told me Tom has always been obsessed by the idea that the Wendleburys stole his birthright, and over the years he told Freddy about it, encouraging him to find out all the details. Freddy told the story to his cousin. Rory had always been clever, but he took every slight personally – his mother calls it sensitive, but I think it was more than that. She says he was often in trouble at school for fighting with anyone he thought had "dissed him", as he put it. He couldn't bear to be overlooked or ignored. That explains why he was so furious when he thought Charlie was stealing his work.'

She took a sip of water, her throat dry. 'Rory left London, cleaned himself up and went to university, taking a BA in anthropology and history before starting a PhD under Charlie's guidance – all linked to his growing obsession with the injustice done to Freddy's family. But he soon grew to resent Charlie's success in the field. Still fascinated by Freddy's history, he was thrilled when the monk's bones turned up.' She sighed. 'He talked to Tom about it, and of course, Tom passed on all his wild, half-baked theories about being the rightful lord of the manor.'

Angela said, 'Although the theories weren't that wild, at all. Tom's – and Freddy's – ancestor, our monk Bernard, really did know the Wendleburys bribed their way to preferment. I bet it was a Wendlebury ancestor who knocked that hole in our monk's head, to keep him quiet.'

ADS Gemma stepped in, 'We searched the manor and found the financial records Rory was looking for, hidden in a priest hole. He didn't find them – I suppose he was in a hurry to finish the search after shooting Mr Wendlebury. Those records showed a sizable transfer of cash from Wendlebury to the Court of Augmentations – far more than the official price of the land. According to historical accounts, Sir Richard Rich, one of Henry VIII's henchmen, was easily bribed.'

Marjorie spoke thoughtfully. 'So, Wendlebury's ancestor killed Bernard to shut him up?'

Gemma shrugged. 'We can't be sure, but that's what Rory decided.'

'We also found the document he stole from the museum in his flat,' Gemma went on. 'The Bill of Sale. And when we looked more carefully, we could see that another buyer's name had originally been written in, and then scratched out, with Wendlebury written over the top. We've sent it away for analysis, and that will take a while, but we're almost sure the first letter of the name was R. It was hard to make it out – it was one of those curly letters they used in those days, and very faint.'

Libby said, 'I bet the other name was Reeves. And that will strengthen our theory that a sixteenth-century Reeves originally bought the land, but a Wendlebury came along and gazumped him with a nice juicy bribe. So, it's very likely our monk, Bernard Reeves as I suppose we could call him, found out and left that angry accusation in the document he was illuminating. And that led to his death, probably at the hands of a Wendlebury.'

There was a long pause, while the members of the society absorbed the information.

Jemima said, 'I thought I saw something – something odd at the abbey, that night.' She hesitated. 'At the time I thought it could have been a monk moving towards the gatehouse, just after midnight, but it could have been Rory on the way to attack Mandy – although he thought it was Charlie – oh dear, what a tangled web it all is.' She clasped her hands together. 'If only I'd called out at the time. I could have saved Mandy.'

Archie Phillips, on her left side, took her hand. 'It's not your fault. We all imagined things, that night. I almost believed I saw a monk in the refectory, but I'm sure he wasn't really there.'

Quentin said, 'Anyway, no one could have arrived at the gate-house in time to stop Rory attacking Mandy.'

William Halfstead said, 'I can understand that Rory burgled the manor and the museum, searching for proof that the manor should have been Freddy's, but that doesn't tell us why he attacked Mandy.'

Charlie raised her hand. 'Let me explain,' she said. 'Because it's partly my fault. You see, I was so excited about our monk and the possible crime his bones suggested that I didn't include Rory in my plans, as I should have done.' She bit her lip. 'I feel ashamed, because I was behaving like one of those old university dons, claiming their students' work as their own. I can't blame Rory for being angry with me, but I had no idea he was such a cold-blooded, calculating creature.' She took a deep breath, avoiding Libby's eyes as she confessed, 'He was right, really. I wasn't exactly stealing his work, but I was planning to put a paper out in my name and he couldn't stand it. I don't know whether he wanted to kill me, or just teach me a lesson...'

Gemma said, 'It fits with his history of fighting at school, taking offence easily, planning revenge...'

William was nodding. 'I wouldn't be surprised to hear he's a psychopath. When I was a schoolteacher, I was told that thirty per cent of the population have psychopathic traits.'

Marjorie shivered. 'That's frightening.'

William squeezed her hand. 'Not everyone with those tendencies ends up killing people. There's no need to panic. But it explains why Rory might have tried to kill Charlie, who hadn't done him any real harm, and why he didn't care whether or not he shot Mr Wendlebury when he burgled Priory Manor.'

Charlie was nodding in agreement. 'Rory came to the ghost hunt with the note already prepared. I think he'd overheard me talking to Max about my paper. I don't think he wanted to kill me – I really need to believe that. I think he just wanted to take out all his anger on me.'

William was puzzled. 'But why attack Mandy?'

Libby said, 'That was a mistake. It was dark, and the night air was chilly. Everyone huddled into blankets and capes, and from behind, Mandy and Charlie look surprisingly similar. Rory tried to lure Charlie into the gatehouse—'

Charlie added, 'He knew I wouldn't be able to resist the promise of information in the note.'

'That's right,' Libby agreed. 'But he put the note in Mandy's pocket by mistake. It was dark, the two of you look alike from behind – and Rory's colour-blind. When Max and I were admiring Rosalind's garden, she told us Rory's father couldn't tell colours apart. Well, colour blindness runs in families. Mandy wore a red cloak, while you had a green blanket around your shoulders, Charlie. The colours looked the same to Rory. Mandy thought the note was meant for her and went to the gatehouse, where he attacked her from behind.'

Angela said, 'So, was Rory the unknown sender of that Get Well Soon card?'

'He was,' Gemma said. She snorted. 'He says he felt "embarrassed" about attacking the wrong person; embarrassed, I suppose, that he made a mistake. He hated the idea he could ever be wrong. He seems to think the card makes up for it. He said, "Well, she didn't die, did she? What's all the fuss about?"'

Libby could hardly speak for a sudden burst of anger. 'In fact, he's still blaming other people for these dreadful things he's done.'

Gemma said, 'I'm afraid so. He's confessed to it all, but he feels no remorse for any of it. That pathological chip on his shoulder's bigger than Priory Manor.'

53

Libby took Bear to the hospital, next day. To her delight, she found Mandy sitting in a chair beside her bed.

'You look pleased with yourself.'

'Yes, home tomorrow. Mum in Bristol.'

'Your speech is coming on,' Libby observed. Although Mandy still spoke carefully and slowly, often searching for the right words, at least she could hold a short conversation.

Mandy nodded vigorously. 'Perfect, soon.' And for the first time, Libby saw the old Mandy beaming at her.

'Mandy,' Libby ventured, 'have you remembered what happened that night, yet?'

Mandy put her fingers to her lips. 'Don't tell Steve. Don't want to upset him. But the note. I thought was Reg.'

'And do you wish it was?'

Mandy laughed. 'No. Reg is my friend, no more. He visit me here, one time. But, Steve and me...' she held up her hands, the fingers and thumbs touching to make a heart shape. 'I promise Steve – three months, then London.' Suddenly, she blushed crimson. 'Steve asked me to marry.'

Libby gasped with delight. 'Did he kneel beside the bed?'

'Not likely,' Mandy chuckled. 'He just... mentioned.'

'And do you want to marry Steve?'

Mandy giggled again. 'I think about it.'

'Well, you can't say life is boring.' Libby and Max were home in Exham-on-Sea, curled up on the sofa in Max's study, a bottle of Pinot on the table, two dogs and a cat snoring at their feet. 'Although, sometimes I wish it was.'

'Do you know what I wish?' Max asked, his stomach tight.

She shook her head.

'I wish I was clever with words. Clever enough to tell you exactly how I feel about you. Because,' he took a breath and plunged in, 'I love you very much, Libby. I know I talked about Charlie too much, but I never felt anything for her beyond admiration and envy for the size of her brain. You always had reservations about her, didn't you?'

Libby interrupted. 'I wasn't jealous, you know. I was just teasing you. I think Charlie has a lot of growing up to do. She may be clever academically, but that's no excuse for using a student to further her own career. Let's hope this has taught her a lesson. I'm hoping her romance with Reg will fizzle out, because he needs someone very special.'

'I think Charlie has her eyes on this Derek from Manchester,'

Max said. 'Anyway, I was about to pay you a compliment. You'd never have treated someone the way she treated Rory. I remember her telling me about the paper she was going to write. She'd sent Rory out of the room to get coffee and, looking back, I think that was deliberate. No wonder he felt pushed aside. He'd made the breakthrough with Bernard's bones, uncovering the man's work in the abbey, and she wanted all the credit.'

'Taking credit for your student's work is no excuse for the student to attack you, though.'

'Of course not. If it were, I bet there'd be a trail of dead professors littering some of our great universities. But Rory was already eaten up with anger and self-pity, thinking the world was against him and his family. Everything in his life made him that way – his parents seem to live almost separate lives, with his dad working long hours or in the garden, while Rosalind feels lonely and comforts herself by obsessing about ghosts and the paranormal and building her career in television.' He sighed. 'Young Rory could have done so well in life, if he hadn't been so sure everyone was against him. His attempt to attack Charlie had failed, so he tried to pre-empt her paper by researching and writing his own book. The police found a rough draft of a proposal to a publisher in his room.'

Libby said, 'That's why he burgled both Priory Manor and the Watchet Museum on the same night. He was working round the clock, conducting his own research, feverishly trying to get in before Charlie. As you say, he's very bright, intellectually. But with terrible, fatal flaws.'

Max swallowed a handful of nuts, while Libby poured another glass of wine.

She held her head on one side, still thinking. 'His Uncle Tom's fixation on fighting "for Freddy" over the new houses didn't help Rory, did it? I hope Tom and Winifred recover from all this.

Maybe Tom will let this old hatred of the Wendleburys go. He came very close to taking the blame for Rory's crimes. While he was pub-crawling around Somerset, according to his statement to the police, moaning about the Wendlebury building plans, his nephew was shooting the poor man dead. Poor, bumbling, not-very-bright Chesterton. It's his funeral in a couple of days, you know.'

'We must go,' Max said.

'Absolutely. I think the entire History Society will be there for him. He deserves a decent send-off, despite all his faults. I gather his politician cousin will give the eulogy.'

Max rolled his eyes and emptied the last drops of wine into his glass. 'That's all we need – a politician's ramblings.' He held Libby closer. 'And then, there's Mandy.'

Her face hardened. 'I'll never forgive Rory for what he did to her. I hope the judge throws the book at him. At least she's getting better, slowly, but it could be months before she's back to normal again and she could have died.' She paused. 'There's one more thing, Max. Do you remember, just before Steve found Mandy in the gatehouse, we all went up to the refectory. It was suddenly cold and I could almost swear I saw something. Not a ghost exactly, but some kind of swirling dust...'

Max was nodding. 'I saw it too and like you I don't know what it was. But that's not all. Just before, Jemima had thought she saw someone moving towards the gatehouse.'

'So she did. I'd forgotten that. She said it wore a monk's cowl – but it could have been Rory. He had a hoodie with him, that night, as well as his baseball cap.' She shivered at the memory. 'I don't suppose we'll ever know. Rosalind will be in big trouble as an accessory to Rory's attack on Mandy and she won't be making her programme – and I shall be surprised if she ever appears on TV again once the story gets out.'

'So, that's another life that Rory's ruined - his own mother's. The damage done by murder just goes on and on, doesn't it?'

Libby nodded. 'Down the years, history repeats itself; the murder of our monk at the abbey, hundreds of years ago, eventually leading to the murder of Chesterton Wendlebury.' She thought for a moment. 'I wonder if Jemima did see a monk near the gatehouse after all. You know, watching over Mandy so she didn't die? It sounds fanciful, but we all thought we saw something odd in the refectory. Maybe the monks wanted us to solve the murder that took place all those years ago.'

Max smiled. 'You're beginning to sound like Cleeva Clapp, herself. And who am I to say you're wrong? But I don't think we'll go ghost hunting again in a hurry.'

ACKNOWLEDGMENTS

Researching and writing *Murder at the Abbey* has been a delight, mostly due to the abbey itself.

One of Somerset's hidden gems, it rests in an idyllic rural setting in West Somerset, and is the perfect spot for a picnic. There's even a handy pub just along the lane.

Much of the abbey is well-preserved, despite Henry VIII's dissolution of the monasteries in England under the auspices of the Court of Augmentations, set up in 1536. It retains the sense of calm serenity loved by Cleeva Clapp, who lived there in the twentieth century and took visitors on tours, selling her own pamphlet which was printed locally by Cox Sons and Co in Williton, for sixpence. I was lucky enough to track down, and now own, a copy of the leaflet in which she neither confirms nor denies the existence of ghosts at the abbey, but mentions 'a strong feeling of unseen power,' writing that 'never once has it been in any way evil'.

I'm indebted not just to Cleeva Clapp, but also to the knowledgeable staff and volunteers from English Heritage, who kindly shared their vast knowledge of Cleeve Abbey and answered any questions helpfully.

The story in *Murder at the Abbey* is fictional, as are the 'documents' that draw Libby and her friends through the mystery, but I've kept to historical facts where evidence exists.

There were thirteen monks at the abbey when it was dissolved, and the fate of several was never known.

Lapis lazuli, as described in the story, has been discovered on a skeleton by University of York archaeologist Anita Radini. She found it on the teeth of a nun who was probably engaged in manuscript illumination.

As always, I'm grateful to the enthusiastic team at Boldwood Books, especially to my editor Caroline, to Jade, my copy editor, and Emily, my proof reader.

And mostly, as always, I want to thank my husband, David, who looks after me while I live in the strange world of my own made-up stories and never complains when I fail to hear a word he says. None of my books would ever be finished without him.

MORE FROM FRANCES EVESHAM

We hope you enjoyed reading *Murder at the Abbey*. If you did, please leave a review.

If you'd like to gift a copy, this book is also available as an ebook, digital audio download and audiobook CD.

Sign up to become a Frances Evesham VIP and receive a free copy of the Lazy Gardener's Cheat Sheet. You will also receive news, competitions and updates on future books:

https://bit.ly/FrancesEveshamSignUp

Discover more about the world of Frances Evesham by visiting boldwoodbooks.com/worldoffrancesevesham

ALSO BY FRANCES EVESHAM

The Exham-On-Sea Murder Mysteries

Murder at the Lighthouse

Murder on the Levels

Murder on the Tor

Murder at the Cathedral

Murder at the Bridge

Murder at the Castle

Murder at the Gorge

Murder at the Abbey

The Ham Hill Murder Mysteries

A Village Murder

A Racing Murder

ABOUT THE AUTHOR

Frances Evesham is the author of the hugely successful Exham-on-Sea Murder Mysteries set in her home county of Somerset. In her spare time, she collects poison recipes and other ways of dispatching her unfortunate victims. She likes to cook with a glass of wine in one hand and a bunch of chillies in the other, her head full of murder—fictional only.

Visit Frances's website: www.francesevesham.com

Follow Frances on social media:

 facebook.com/frances.evesham.writer

twitter.com/FrancesEvesham

instagram.com/francesevesham

bookbub.com/authors/frances-evesham

ABOUT BOLDWOOD BOOKS

Boldwood Books is a fiction publishing company seeking out the best stories from around the world.

Find out more at www.boldwoodbooks.com

Sign up to the Book and Tonic newsletter for news, offers and competitions from Boldwood Books!

http://www.bit.ly/bookandtonic

We'd love to hear from you, follow us on social media:

facebook.com/BookandTonic

twitter.com/BoldwoodBooks

instagram.com/BookandTonic

Printed in Great Britain
by Amazon

79691273R00149